)-MO-LOCO

BOOK # 1

THE INK MONKEY & HER SQUONK

BY

SOVANN SOMRETH

Visit Wishy-Wishy on Facebook:
@Wishywishywocomoloco

From Kirkus Review:

A girl with an unpronounceable name discovers that she can use wordplay to change other people's destinies in Somreth's middle-grade novel.

Jane Doe Smith has been raised on word games by Mommy Dee and Daddy Joe in a double-decker bus among the swamps of Okefenokee, Georgia. When she starts attending the labyrinthine Lewis Middle School, she hopes only to avoid her bully, Ezequio. However, after Jane discovers on the first day of school that her legal name is actually Ouishiouishiwocomoloceau (pronounced as in the book's title), Ezequio smears mud on her face. Jane --now known as "Wishy-Wishy"--then finds that invoking her true name allows her to transform people into mythical creatures. As a result, Ezequio becomes a "*squonk*," a pitiable beast who can't stop weeping, hates the sun, and, oddly enough, reads Walt Whitman.

Remorseful but unable to reverse the curse, Wishy-Wishy tries to adjust to middle school life by studying grammar with her only friend, the brilliant Indian foreign exchange student Adhyaksa, in a remedial English class taught by Principal Mathis. Mathis encourages students to get C's, forces them to write shorthand in crayon, and tells bad jokes that strangely seem to make him shrink when he tells them. The fearsome Jabberwock, who's long stalked children from Lewis Middle School's Gifted and Talented Education program, perceives Adhyaksa's intelligence and imagination and abducts her in order to steal her dreams. Newly friendless Wishy-Wishy tries to remember

Adhyaksa when nobody else can while Spanish-language peer tutors, who may actually be Naga snakes, stalk her.

This allusion-packed, lyrical, and thoroughly absurdist fantasy has aspects that some readers will find reminiscent of Louis Sachar's Wayside Schoolbooks. However, something more romantic and experimental bubbles beneath its surface. Although toilet humor and one-off rhyming wordplay abound, other scenes ring with existential resonance, as when Ezequio mourns his dead mother's lettuce preference or the Jabberwock monologues triumphantly about Principal Mathis' growing financial debt. Each unpredictable reveal deepens the unreality, but Wishy-Wishy's gradual mastery of her powers feels earned, and the book's bracing balance of silliness, alliteration, and high stakes will engage readers.

A head-spinning yarn that captures the magic, horror, and silliness of late childhood.

Plain Jane Doe Smith learns sometimes a plain name suits one just fine.

Jane Doe Smith is not content with her plain Jane name. Though she lives in a re-purposed double-decker bus, complete with all necessary amenities and exciting adventures, the question of her name seems to be her greatest torment. Imagine her surprise when she returns to school to find out she has another legal name; the one her parents have been sparing her from for years: Ouishiouishiwocomoloceau. This new name unleashes a world of trouble for young Jane. Her classmates tease her and she finds even she is unable to spell it. Despite her bookish nature, her failure to spell her name lands her in a remedial English class where students are encouraged to get barely passing grades and complete all assignments in crayon. What's worse, Jane discovers she now has the power to turn people into mythical creatures, provided they are able to say her real name, and that she gives them a rhyming nickname in kind. This just might come in handy when a nonsensical Jabberwock comes to her Middle School to feed on the imaginations of children.

Sovann Somreth's *Wishy-Wishy-Woco-Mo-Loco: The Ink Monkey and Her Squonk* is, of course, a total mouthful of a title. The story itself is absolutely charming and a fun series of pages of word play and absurdity. The book is best designed for young readers in middle school, but it is also an absolute treat for their parents who enjoy silly wordplay. For those who remember the *Amelia Bedelia* books, this book is similar in comparison with its rhyming words, but the misunderstandings and wordplay in Somreth's work seems far less destructive.

The charming story of how this book came to be should also be told. Writer Sovann Somreth was flipping through his daughter's yearbook with her. She bemoaned the fact that she felt she had such a normal name and would have loved a fancier one. Her parents jokingly told her that they'd almost named her Ouishiouishiwocomoloceau, and the idea for this charming story was born.

-Victoria Irwin
Editor in Chief of FangirlNation.com

TABLE OF CONTENTS

* * *

For Lydia & Aaron

CHAPTER 1

THE COMMODORE

The Smiths lived in a double-decker bus along the swamps of Okefenokee. In their house on wheels, they had everything they needed: a tiny kitchen to fix up supper, a cozy bedroom for Daddy Joe and Mommy Dee, a loft for Jane, and a ten-gallon aquarium for her rainbow fish. They pared down everything they owned, even their names.

Jane, however, wasn't always happy with her name. She sat in her reading nook and thumbed through her 5th grade yearbook. She peeked up from the mosaic cover and said, "Daddy Joe, why didn't you name me something fancy, like Portia or Victoria or Nancy? I had an Isabella in my class. Her name means beautiful island."

Jane turned to her aquarium and fed her pair of rainbow fish. "How are you doing, Bob-Betsy and Bob-Bella?" She capped the flakes then went on, "I first met Peter on the swing during recess. His gums had a great big abscess. I met Annabelle after P.E.

when I needed to pee. We raced to the bathroom. She can run much faster than me."

She turned a few pages. "In class, I sat next to a boy named Rahil. His desk is by the window sill. He plays the piano. He's already been to Katmandu and Timbuktu. And then there's me. I've been to the mall and maybe the zoo."

Jane closed her yearbook. "There's a boy, Ezequio. He has the coolest name of all. He also has a habit of stealing my lunch money. Not because he needs it, but because he likes to tear it in two. 'One for me and one for you,' he would say."

"Maybe it's his way of sharing," said Mommy Dee.

"He is so annoying." Jane slid down the firemen's pole, plunked herself on the sofa and scowled. "And then there's you, Daddy Joe. Are you okay with being an average Joe with a simple name?"

"You might say I live a low-key kind of life," Daddy Joe said. He liked to keep to himself, working away in his shed, making a bookshelf or a bed in his A-frame wood shop on wheels.

Jane unfolded up her hemlock craft table, dropped the legs, and snapped a few latches into place. Then she folded down a hurdy-gurdy from a recess in the wall. "Jane Doe Smith. You can find me on any paper form. I am the unnamed witness of every crime.

2

She gave the crank arm on her musical instrument a constant turn and massaged the keys.

I am super incognito,
a bowl of mashed potatoes
served up everyday

They never ask me where I come from
think my road in life's a humdrum
each and every way

It's just me, Bob-Betsy and Bob-Bella
I don't know who's the fella
I love them come what may

Please don't spare me the paprika
I'd really like to meet ya
and listen to what you say

We can turn the hurdy-gurdy
If you're feelin' kinda nerdy
We can talk until we're flirty
If you're feelin' kinda wordy

But until you get to know me,
I'll be your mashed potatoes
each and everyday.

❆ ❆ ❆

…Tell me, Daddy Joe. Should I donate my body to science? I have the perfect name for a cadaver."

"Over my dead body," said Mommy Dee. She grabbed an oven mitt, took the banana bread out of the oven, and placed it on a crockery to rest.

"Sounds like a two for one special," said Daddy Joe. He took off his ranger hat and tried to explain, "You see. Your Mommy Dee and me…we were wishy-washy. We couldn't make up our minds. Chancing upon your name made us plum-loco. So when you woke, we called you Jane." With those words, he grabbed the Sunday paper and took his spot at the helm.

"I wish my name wasn't so plain," Jane said.

"Don't we all," said Mommy Dee. "Do you want to change it?"

"No. Don't bother. I'm just being silly."

"Tell me more about this Ezequio. What else did he do?"

"He likes to pick on me and mostly me. He can be such a meanie. Besides half my lunch money, he also steals half my homework, tears out the answers he doesn't even need."

"How polite," said Mommy Dee.

"He will call me names and do it with a grin. And

I'm not as clumsy as you might think. Whenever you saw dirt on my shirt or an obnoxious shade of ink, it was Ezequio, I think you should know. And when I nearly won the 5th grade spelling bee, he poured chocolate milk all over me."

"What was the winning word?"

"Schadenfreude." Jane let out an exasperated sigh. "Finding joy in the misfortune of others. I made the mistake of asking for an example, and he was happy to oblige."

"Why haven't you told me any of these things before?"

"You never asked. Do you want to know more?"

"That's quite enough."

Mommy Dee asked Jane to follow into her room. She looked out the window and saw the strato-marshmallow clouds. "There will come soft rain. Tomorrow is the first day of school, and I want you looking prim. I think you have grown enough to fit your grandma's dress."

Jane imagined a formaldehyde leeching trunk filled with mothballs. Her mother must have kept it in secret for the longest time so that she could reveal this family heirloom in all its glory.

Mommy Dee instead pulled out a drawer from under the bed. There was no need for mothballs. She kept the dress in a vacuum-sealed bag to save space. The bag hissed and filled with air as she broke the seal. There was no need to fret for Jane's grandmother had impeccable taste. It was inexplicably modern and chic. The dress fit Jane perfectly without any mending. She walked around the house and gave herself a twirl. "If it were shorter, and had some ruffles, I'd look like a Harajuku girl," Jane said. She changed out of the dress and placed it at her bedside. It was far too nice to wear around the house.

Jane broke out morsels of banana bread and stuffed her cheeks until they could chub no more. Then she added some sweet butter that she had made with her homemade, hand-cranked butter churn. It gave her palms some callouses but was well worth the effort.

Living in a double-decker bus was not all glamour. Her chores included checking the air pressure and hosing the windows with a pressure washer. It wasn't their first tiny house. The previous one had no wheels and was half the current size. Back then Daddy Joe was learning the trade. But there was nothing he couldn't figure out with imagination and sweat equity, and by the time Jane turned 12, he had created a masterpiece and christened it with a bottle of bubbly apple cider. For a tiny home, The Commodore, as

Jane affectionately called it, was ample in every way. Reddish brown on top, blue on the bottom, it looked as if it was ready to sail the high seas.

CHAPTER 2

THE HOKEY POKEY

It was a new school year at Lewis Middle School. Jane hugged Daddy Joe goodbye and made haste to her classroom. The sprawling campus could have easily handled a high school population, though only every other classroom was in use and those that were in use did not look particularly inspiring. If anything, they looked like cottages with their inner walls knocked out. The middle school encompassed mostly the western cluster of stand-alone buildings that enclosed a field of grass known as the quad. A network of overhangs shielded the student body from the rain and sun while paver stones below formed the walkways.

Now about the dress. Jane was fine with what she wore until she saw she was the only one dressed like she had a dance to attend. On a rainy day when everyone wore drab colors of black, blue or gray, the dress she wore to look her best, at mommy Dee's behest, was a daffodil yellow with semi-circles around the collar. It turned heads and caused the occasional bump into a wall from boys not looking where they were going.

"Why would Mommy Dee do this to me?" Jane said.

She spotted Ezequio and made sure to veer another way. He was too busy retying his Chuck Taylor shoes to notice. He had grown quite a bit, and with his Paul Bunyan flannel shirt, seemed better dressed than she remembered.

Jane darted straight across the quad and into her classroom. She found a chair in the back corner of the room and cowered like a platypus under her knapsack.

Her social studies teacher -Mrs. Figgelworth took attendance. Jane was relieved not to see Ezequio in class. There will be the usual Sarah, Emily, and Jane, Jane thought. Then came the fancier names. Her teacher read through Adhyaksa, Balthazar, and Zepherine. Not to mention the occasional odd name like Stephanie Biggle. Not that she was a big girl or anything.

When Mrs. Figgleworth got to Jane, she took a pause. Mrs. Figgelworth puckered her lips twice, tried to sound it out.

It shouldn't be so hard Jane thought. I have the easiest name in the world. "It's Jane. Plain Jane

Smith," she said to her teacher.

Mrs. Figgelworth gave her an odd look and picked up her puny purple marker. She wrote Jane's name on the board; only Jane wasn't what she wrote.

Ouishiouishiwocomoloceau Smith

"Let's see," said Mrs. Figgelworth while pushing her horn-rimmed spectacles above the mole on her nose. "The first part looks either French or Japanese. The middle part looks Sub-Saharan. The last part may be Latin? How can someone with such a common family name have such a...special name? How do you pronounce your name, young lady?"

Jane noodled long and hard about what Daddy Joe told her the day before. Let's see. My parents were wishy-washy. Coming up with my name made them plum-loco. When I woke, they called me Jane, but my real name must be "Wishy-wishy-woco-mo-loco." She didn't realize she said her name aloud.

"Of course that's how you say it. What a lovely name" said Mrs. Figgelworth.

Before Jane or shall we say Wishy-Wishy knew it, her name caught on. One student after another repeated the chant:

Wishy-wishy-woco-mo-loco
Wishy-wishy-woco-mo-loco

"What a catchy name," Jason jested. "Try it, Spencer. It's so slippery. It just rolls off the tongue."

"It sounds weird," Mackenzie mentioned. "She must be weird."

"I think it's full of wishes," Balthazar blasted. "Although parts of it look suspicious. How did she ever survive fifth grade?"

Wishy-Wishy wanted to shrivel into the recesses of a cone snail shell until no one could poke her with a toothpick. They would have bend it first. Although she despised her name, she seethed when Lucretia Chen mispronounced it. She hissed through her teeth, "It's Wishy-Wishy, not Ooshi-Ooshi, you unwitty-twitty."

She struggled to spell out her name on classroom assignments. She gave up on her reading assessment test because she didn't have room to type it in. The only comfort she felt was when Mrs. Figgelworth wanted to call on her to read a passage out of a book but then thought better of it. Wishy-wishy dared not raise her hand when Mrs. Figgelworth asked the class who was first to challenge the notion of an earth-centered universe, even though Wishy-Wishy knew it.

"Copernicus," said Mrs. Figgelworth. "Alright, class. It's time for some stretching because sitting down too much will kill you. Today we'll dance the hokey-pokey."

Nobody wanted to dance the hokey pokey with Wishy-Wishy from Okefenokee.

CHAPTER 3

MR. MATHIS

At lunch, she ran into him near the drinking fountain. Or rather, he ran into her. Ezequio started from afar. He floated down from a mound, picked up speed and gave it a good sprint. Her dress he muddled when he landed on a puddle.

"I heard you have a new name," said Ezequio.

It befuddled Wishy-Wishy how the news had spread so quickly.

"Don't say it," she said.

"Say what? Wishy-wishy-woco-mo-loco?"

"That's my name, don't wear it out," Wishy-Wishy said soberly.

"Miss I think I'm going loco?" He picked up a cold handful of mud. "Think you're special?"

"I know I am, but what are you?" She couldn't think of anything clever to say.

"Think a fancy name and a fancy dress will give you friends?" He smeared it on her cheek. But when he tried to pull out his hand, she held it there.

Wishy-Wishy closed her eyes. She wished she was in another place, that the hand belonged to an innocent boy, that Ezequio, of all people, could possibly be her friend.

She opened her eyes. "Sticks and stones may break my bones, but mud can never hurt me, Ezequio Radicchio." She cast his hand away.

"What did you call me?"

"Ezequio Radicchio. I only said it because it rhymed."

"No one ever called me that." He fell to his knees. "It's just that my mother used to pack radicchio in my lunch. Always hated radicchio. But now that it's gone, it's all I've ever wanted."

He wanted to tell her more but didn't know how to put it into words. He saw the mud on her face, the facets in her eyes and cried.

Radicchio must mean a lot to Ezequio, Wishy-Wishy thought.

"I'm so sorry," she said.

Just as she reached out with her hand, a hall monitor pinched Ezequio's ear and dragged him along. He looked back at her and winced.

Wishy-Wishy found herself in the nearest bathroom and rinsed off her face over the sink. It was the kind of faucet she had to press every ten seconds.

14

She wasn't sure what just happened. She wondered why Ezequio's mom couldn't go to the nearest farmer's market and buy some more red-leafed radicchio, mix it up with some romaine lettuce to break up the monotony. She stepped outside and wanted to settle into a remote corner of a round quad, if there ever was such a place, anywhere to avoid classmates who knew her name. Only then did she notice her heart race. Maybe it was the way Ezequio said things. For some odd reason, she couldn't help but cry as well. She felt a shortness of breath, reached for her asthma inhaler and took in a spritz.

Moments later, a voice blared out on the public announcement system, "This is Principal Mathis. Will Wishy-wishy-woco-mo-loco, I mean Jane Smith, please report to my office? Calling on Wishy-Wishy, I mean Jane Smith…"

It was only right that Wishy-Wishy would end up in the principle's office on the first day of school. She walked misty-eyed across campus while other students filed back into class. Wishy-Wishy imagined she would have to stay late and write her cumbersome name a hundred times on an old dusty chalkboard, even though the school no longer had any old dusty chalkboards. They would somehow pull it out of retirement to punish her for having such a weird name and then tuck it neatly away for safekeeping until a Madagascan boy would take her crown away.

The office was poorly lit and smelled of half-eaten candy, Reeses Pieces, to be precise. Sitting in the corner was a kid sucking on his thumb with a dunce cap on his head. He was about the size of an overgrown second grader. "Come in Jane," said the kid in a grown man's voice. "I'm Principal Mathis." He had well-coiffured platinum gray hair and a mustache to match. His back hunched. His eyes loomed largely, yet his pupils seemed tiny, like a shrew in winter.

Behind his desk stood a hutch filled to the brim with track and field medals and varsity football trophies with the name Roy Mathis etched for all eternity. She found it odd for such a tiny man.

"What do you call 2.2 pounds of figs?" he asked.

"I don't know," Wishy-Wishy said.

"A fig newton. Get it?" He bit into a fig and let out a giddy laugh at his own corny joke.

"Mr. Mathis?"

"Yes?" he still had the fig between his teeth, half of it in and half of it out.

"I've heard a newton is just shy of a quarter-pound," she said in a faint, demur tone.

He opened his eyes wide and said through the fig,

"It is?"

"You would only need that much fig and it would have to be falling to make a newton of force."

He bit through the fig. Half of it landed squish on the floor, producing half a fig newton. He seemed to shrink in his chair. "I hate it when my joke falls flat." He fiddled with the knobs below his rickety seat. "You know I've always had a few screws loose." The chair rose two inches. "Where did you learn that sort of thing?"

"My Daddy Joe," Wishy-Wishy said without hesitation. "He's a simple man. He makes not so simple things so simple and tells me about the simple things that are not so simple. He tells me useful useless stuff," she added with a nod.

"I wish somebody would have told me sooner. They always laugh along or let it slide just because I'm the principal." He let out a sigh and pointed to the top of his head. "Like my hat? Made it myself."

"What are you doing?" asked Wishy-Wishy. "I thought they outlawed this sort of thing."

"Yeah, I thought so too. But I did b-a-a-a-d thing," said Principal Mathis. "And when I do something wrong, I will either flush my foot down the toilet, stand on my head, or what you are seeing right now." His eyes roamed around. "How do I explain this. It was about the time we were putting together the classroom rosters. Your momma told me to take special care with your name, but I goofed." Principle Mathis straightened out his dunce cap then went on, "How did it happen? Let's see. I was at the drive-through last week when she phoned me. I could barely make out what she was saying from all the honky-tonk coming from the car behind me. I was trying to decide between something plain like house blend, half-caf/decaf, or the swiss-miss-caramel-mocha-tapioca-cappuccino-macchiato when your momma told me to call you Jane and not Wishy-wishy-woco-mo-loco. Needless to say, I went with the fancy one and you know the rest." He patted his plump tummy.

Wishy-Wishy took a moment to digest.

Principal Mathis removed his hat, walked over to his desk and grabbed the microphone. "Do you want me to tell everyone to call you Jane Smith? I can serve an automatic detention to anyone who makes fun of your name."

Wishy-Wishy imagined a popcorn serving gymnasium full of rowdy kids impatiently staring at a clock projected on a jumbotron screen and Principal Mathis standing atop a ladder shouting through a megaphone, telling everyone to pipe down. Then she saw Ezequio in the middle of the floor, sitting on the only desk. He had his head down, buried in his arms.

"It's no use," She said. "From this moment on, my name is Wishy-wishy-woco-mo-loco, but you can call me L'il Ms. Smith or Squishy-Fishy-Wishy-Wishy. I don't care anymore."

Principal Mathis sent Wishy-Wishy back to class.

"Try not to make the news…" he said as the door closed. He reached into his candy jar and pulled out a Snicker-snack, chewed thoughtfully, then chased it down with a pair of Tums from a glass jar shaped like a Christmas tree. He liked to call it his Tum-Tum tree. "What to do with this Ezequio," he muttered to himself.

In the next room sat Ezequio. He had gathered himself. He looked at the hand he hadn't washed and thought about Wishy-Wishy and the yellow dress he muddled. He didn't think he could ever look her in the eyes again. If he had to do it all over again, he would have done the same. It was only right that he rubbed mud on her face. He had to do it. No one else knew any better. She didn't deserve it. She needed it.

A minute later, Principal Mathis picked up the phone and called his office manager to send Ezequio in.

Ezequio stepped in from a nearby office and had a

seat.

"What do you call a prison term when it won't end and it just seems to go on and on and it just won't end?" asked Mr. Mathis.

Ezequio shook his head.

"A run-on sentence." Mr. Mathis snickered uneasily and waited to see if his joke stuck the landing. It was okay if the joke vaulted over Ezequio's head, or if Ezequio wasn't in the mood to laugh, but he could ill afford another embarrassing correction. He adjusted his four-inch seat cushion and went on. "You know I have no tolerance when it comes to bullying and name-calling, don't you?"

Ezequio nodded.

"And you know the common treatment for such things, don't you?"

Ezequio gulped.

"I have a way of dealing with misfits. Tell me. Do you know who Prometheus was?"

Ezequio shook his head again.

"Prometheus stole fire from the Gods of Mount Olympus and gave it to us mortals, normal people like you and me. Try to keep him in mind the next time you burn the midnight oil." Mr. Mathis leaned up off his seat cushion, locked eyes on Ezequio and said in a demanding, yet caring whisper, "Now son, I want you to go to the library on the hill. And then I want you to steal whatever books you want, as many as you want, as much as your arms can hold." There was a quivering sense of urgency in his voice like time was running out and the fate of mankind depended on it.

"Why can't I just borrow it?" asked Ezequio, not that he had ever checked out a book.

"It won't be the same. It just won't be the same," whispered Mr. Mathis. He raised his brows. "Think of the risk. Think of the prize. Think of the surprise in your eyes if they catch you with /The Catcher in the Rye/." He crossed his eyes (ⓒ ⟆ ⊃) then shook it off.

Ezequio knew every book had a little chip that would set off alarms. With classes in session, there would be no one in the library to add to the confusion or use as a cover.

"How will I get past the Librarians?" Ezequio asked.

"Oh yes, that part." Mr. Mathis fumbled inside his desk and pulled out a paper triangle football he had confiscated for himself. "You have only one of these so use it wisely. Go in through the back. They're counting books and balancing the books to start out the year. The door will be open. If you should run into any trouble, throw the football at their feet. When they see it, say 'Nick-nack-patty-whack!' and they will freeze in place. If you should see a guard dog, then give it a bone. And when you're done, you go on running home."

"I don't think it will work, Mr. Mathis."

"For your sake, Ezequio, you better hope it does."

After Ezequio had gone, Mr. Mathis picked up his phone and called the librarian. "This is Principal Mathis. I have a young gentleman in a flannel shirt who will pay a visit. Give him some space, if you know what I mean. And one more thing. Let me know how many books he takes. I will donate 2.2 times as much."

Mr. Mathis took the student report on Ezequio, crumbled it up into a ball and threw a sky-hook at the wastebasket. He made a whistling sound as it flew through the air and then a TWOINGOINGIONGIONG sound when the shot bounced off the rim.

Then he looked at the clock. It was his favorite time of day. Ms. Gertrude came by to pick him up. He wore pudgy running shoes just for this occasion. He heard the door open.

"Come to my arms, my beamish boy…"

He ran to her.

She picked him up.

"Weeeeeee!" He chortled in his joy.

Sovann Somreth

CHAPTER 4

BOB-BETSY & BOB-BELLA

Jane wasn't her talkative self on the ride back home. She did not provide her usual play by play recap of the school day. Daddy Joe noticed something was wrong, but he also knew not to pry. He brought the car to a gentle stop next to their home. She rolled her carcass out of the Jeep and dragged her feet as she made her way into the bus-house. She left her knapsack on the passenger seat, turned straight to the left and labored herself up the ladder and into her loft. She liked the small confines of her room whenever her life got too complicated. She tossed her soiled dress down the laundry chute and pressed a button to send a rush of air to swoosh it into the basket below.

Mommy Dee fixed up supper in the galley kitchen below. She reached into a zeer pot fridge and pulled out some bell peppers. A zeer pot fridge was nothing more than a clay pot within another clay pot. Sand and water filled the gap between the pots. Through the basic principles of capillary action and evaporative cooling, the Smiths could keep produce fresh without the need for a larger fridge.

Wishy-Wishy laid in bed with her hands behind her head and looked up at the clouds through her porthole skylight. She could hear raindrops hitting the roof of the bus and the rivulets of water flowing down the solar panels that funneled it into collection barrels. Their house was small, but being able to hear the rain provided a sense of chrysalism, of being safe. Even though it poured outside, she was warm and snug in her down comforter cocoon. She wondered aloud, "Am I a bad person?"

"Of course not," said Mommy Dee.

"I made a boy cry today."

"That doesn't happen often," replied her mother.

"Do you know what else happened today?"

"Mr. Mathis called and apologized about your name."

"People shouldn't have to apologize for saying my name," Wishy-Wishy said. She opened a jar of flakes and fed her rainbow fish. She had the rare ability to read fish lips. Or at least she liked to think she did while feeding her fish. "What do you think, Bob-Betsy and Bob-Bella?"

Bob-Betsy fluoresced beneath her scales. Shimmering pigments of blue and yellow provided a feast for the eyes. She circled the tank then mouthed, "There's a log in a bog with a bunch of pollywogs. There are bees in the trees. Don't disturb them would you please? There is honey for some money and it makes the tea so sweet, what a treat."

"I don't know how you would know what tea or honey tastes like, Bob-Betsy." Then she stumbled on a profound question. "Is it better to have honey for some money or money for some honey?" Wishy-Wishy waited a few minutes then followed the flakes with some tropical pellets.

Bob-Bella swam a somersault then chanted, "There's a girl in the world, and she doesn't like her name —what a shame."

Daddy Joe tucked a new log into the stove. He heard what she sang from above before the stove top kettle came to a boil. He pressed a valve and released the steaming hot water into his mug to dilute the coffee crystals.

He had a seat on the built-in sofa and peered out to the the pitch dark swamp. "I know it might seem odd, but your mommy and me used to live busy worker bee lives, keeping up with the Jones'. The world became too much. That's why we sold our house and kept only what we needed," said Daddy Joe.

"Everything here has meaning to us and not one ounce more," said Mommy Dee.

"Then why is my real name so dang long —and meaningless? If it were to have meaning, it can't be any good," said Wish-wishy.

"Tell me, Jane, are you sad we chose to live this way?" her father asked.

"A little bit. It was easier when you home-schooled me. And I do like our new house on wheels a lot more than the one before. And you can call me Wishy-Wishy from now on," she said.

Mommy Dee pulled down a magnetic spice jar that clung to the tin ceiling. She sprinkled the thyme onto the spaghetti and went on, "To tell you the truth, Ouishiouishiwocomoloceau was the name written on your birth certificate. We called you Jane so that you wouldn't have to put up with the name calling in school."

"Why didn't you officially change it to Jane when you had a chance?" asked Wishy-Wishy.

"I don't know. It never occurred to us," said Mommy Dee.

"It doesn't have to be this way," said Daddy Joe. "You see Jane, Wishy-Wishy, I thought ahead. When I built our tiny house, I made sure it was on wheels. I made sure we had everything we needed. Energy from the sun, water from the rain or garden hose hookup if need be. We are not tied to one place. We can change location as we please. Maybe what's needed is a new start. Maybe what's needed is a change of scenery."

"You mean move?" asked Wishy-Wishy.

"Your wish is my command. We won't have a particular place in mind. We'll catch fireflies along the way. We'll just drive until we feel like stopping."

They packed their belongings before dawn could hiccup a yolk into the night. By then the rain had subsided. Daddy Joe stacked up the plastic chairs and emptied out the composting tanks. Mommy Dee tidied up the tiny house. There wasn't much to clean. They were ready in an hour.

Mommy Dee drove the pickup truck with workshop in tow while Daddy Joe drove the bus-house on wheels. Wishy-Wishy took a seat on the front passenger chair. She knew their house had wheels, but never thought it could actually move. Daddy Joe started up the diesel engine.

"Daddy Joe, for a simple man, you are just full of surprises." Wishy-Wishy said.

They drove 80 yards to the north side of the pond when the engine died. Daddy Joe scratched his head. "I think I forgot about the fuel."

Wishy-Wishy took stock of the new view, how the

willow trees framed the lake on either side and reckoned, "It actually looks better from this side of the pond. Why don't we stay here a while. Besides, I have school today."

CHAPTER 5

REMEDIAL

Ezequio pulled the covers over his bed-head. That day there would be no radicchio in Ezequio's lunch. There would be no school for Ezequio. There would be an empty desk where Ezequio would have sat when Mr. Mathis took attendance during English class.

English was the only class Mr. Mathis taught at Lewis Middle School. It was a remedial class for special students in need of a more attention -which was why a wincing Wishy-Wishy would wrestle with what waning pride was left when she discovered that she had somehow ended up in such a class.

Wishy-Wishy took stock of the room and recognized no one from her previous school. Most of her friends, like Annabelle and Rahil, made it into a normal English class. In their place was a collection of unpopular misfits, too much like herself than she dared to admit.

"This must be a mistake," Wishy-Wishy blurted aloud.

"Not according to the results of your English assessment test," reminded Mr. Mathis. "Not only did you fail your test, but you didn't even spell your name correctly."

"There wasn't enough room!" Wishy-Wishy pouted. She pounded her head on the desk with a THUMP-THUMP-THUMP and kept it down there for a spell.

Wishy-Wishy knew it would be one of those days as soon as she put on her Osh-Kosh overalls and leather clogs earlier that morning. The way her socks bunched up beneath her feet left a crease that was annoying enough to notice but couldn't be bothered to straighten out. What she felt throughout the day was an itch on the ball of her feet that came and went. She wasn't sure if it was from a bug bite or something her mind made up when something was not right in the world.

Wishy-Wishy turned to one side, saw Ezequio's empty desk, and she wondered how awkward it would be when Ezequio shows up the next day. Would she act nonchalant? Pretend the whole ordeal with the mud never happened? She gathered herself and took to coloring a map of the school with crayons.

"It is important you know the layout of our school," Mr. Mathis said. "Students have been known to go missing for days on end and then mysteriously show up the next day as if the days on end never existed. It happens more often than you think."

Lewis Middle School sat across a sprawling campus. It could take 20 minutes to walk from the south end of the campus, where the entrance stood, to the north end, where a donated library perched atop a round hill, surrounded by a labyrinth of hedges. Stray off the beaten path, and one might find oneself late for class. A river looped around the campus from the north and toward the western bend like a semi-circle before continuing south along the entrance road. The classrooms, which were mostly standalone, ran along an outer ring and an inner ring, like two concentric diamonds surrounding a central quad. The athletic fields opened out toward the east, beyond that, vast fields of peanuts and soy. There was an administrative wing along the northeast inner ring where Wishy-Wishy first met Mr. Mathis. His English classroom # 53 sat at the westernmost end of the campus, and when the shades were drawn open, the room had a clear view of the vast swamplands that lie beyond the river. To the northeast lie the forgotten campus where buildings sat in stasis. The stone buildings have held up so well that to walk to this part of campus would be to stumble into a university.

In Mr. Mathis' class, crayons were de rigueur. He forbade sharp writing instruments like mechanical pencils and ballpoint pens. The things people wrote with them were in his words, "Too much on the nose, like shooting kittens with a machine gun when all you need is catnip."

Because crayons are dull, Wishy-Wishy had to know exactly what she wanted to write, before things got too dull, and she had to stop writing. Mr. Mathis allowed the luxury of one sharp yellow No. 2 pencil for the school year, but no sharpening.

"In this day and age of copy and paste, I have to make sure your words are yours and yours alone. To survive in my class," Mr. Mathis explained, "You will have to master shorthand stenography, Braille, or…" Mr. Mathis rolled his eyes, "Morse code. But no matter which method you choose, brevity is key."

It became abundantly clear to Wishy-Wishy that Mr. Mathis' remedial English class was not for ordinary kids. The only way he could teach such useful useless things was to set the bar exceptionally low. In fact, to stay in his class, students had to maintain a C average on all standardized tests. Score too low and risk district intervention. Score too high and risk advancement into a normal English class, where useless useful things are taught.

Oddly enough, after the first two days of class, neither she nor anyone else wanted to do better or worse than average. Mr. Mathis devoted much of class time to storytelling. They had to be tall tales because here was this short guy telling the class how he was the star of the school football team. When he wasn't reminiscing about high school, he would dive into the ancient classics and make them new again. To Wishy-Wishy it sometimes seemed like deja vu, especially when she mouthed the lines to Alfred Lord Tennyson as Mr. Mathis read from his anthology. It was as if she heard the splendor falls on castle walls a long, long time ago, but she couldn't remember when.

Wishy-Wishy took to shorthand and learned how to write her name in this weird style of writing that only courtroom stenographers knew. She signed her name as such on her assignments:

If she thought her name was hard to read at first, shorthand made it even more so. Maybe it was because Adhyaksa too had a hard name to spell and pronounce that the two crossed paths at recess. Adhyaksa admired Wishy-Wishy for standing up to

Ezequio. In Adhyaksa, Wishy-Wishy found her first new friend in school.

Unlike Wishy-Wishy, Adhyaksa was still learning English and was a natural C student in English. Wishy-Wishy needed more help in maintaining a perfect C. She often leaned on Adhyaksa for the wrong answers.

On the fourth day of school, Mr. Mathis' English class took a walk to the library on the hill. They did not stray from the gravel path and to be sure, Mr. Mathis made his students hold on to a rope with 25 knots. The last knot was empty.

"Stay clear from the holly bushes and stay the center course, not too close to Juneau, and not too close to Jove," said Mr. Mathis. Concrete statues of gods and goddesses peeked their heads above the hedgerows.

The library was a well-maintained four-bedroom Victorian house. It had a fresh coat of monkey-vomit-green paint and looked like it could last another 100 years, but not much longer.

Mr. Mathis stood up on a sliding stool and announced, "For your class project, you will need to choose a character from ancient mythology and become that character. You will dress up and act out your character in a skit of sorts with a partner. So get to know your character and your partner well."

They wandered around the library. Samantha Fontaine raced to the second floor and found a book on Atalanta. Timothy Timmons teetered on his tippy toes, trying to take the tale of Tantalus from the top shelf in the attic. He was so tantalizingly close. Adhyaksa Narayamamurti naturally gravitated toward the Indian characters within the Ramayana. And Romona Robbins? She just stared at her rippled reflection on the surface of a koi pond.

The library was devoted to myths of many genres, each with its own heroes and monsters. Because she noticed everyone going for either Greek or Roman characters, which she was all too familiar with, Wishy-Wishy opted for a remote corner of the basement where she found a neglected shelf. The books here weren't on anything in general, but rather, they were bestiaries, collections of random and lesser-known creatures and monsters. She picked out Jorge Luis Borges' /Book of Imaginary Beings/.

Wishy-Wishy finished the book in one sitting that night. She reasoned that most mythical creatures or lessor gods lived such wretched lives. They had great gifts, but the greater Gods often punished them with repetitive things. She imagined herself as the titan Prometheus and dreaded having her liver eaten out each morning by a vulture, only to have it grow back overnight for the vulture to eat again the next morning. Such was Prometheus' punishment for stealing fire from the Gods.

To be the titan Sisyphus would be more of the same, but involve pushing a boulder up a hill. She would work tirelessly and not think of the past nor the future, like the god Janus. Such is the reality she would face if she were to grow up and get a 9 to 5 job with a daily grind and an ugly commute.

Her luck would be no better if she chose to be the river nymph Daphne. Cupid would shoot her with a lead arrow and then shoot Apollo with a golden arrow. She would endlessly run from an infatuated Apollo. Her only option would be to pray for Daddy Joe to turn her into a laurel tree because who could love a laurel tree? Then there was Medusa, who was so beautiful, the goddess Athena turned her into a snake haired gorgon and made her so ugly that men who gazed upon her turned into stone.

At least Wishy-Wishy found a book with innocuous creatures who were better at hiding from the wrath of a jealous god. She chose to be an Ink Monkey for her skit. An Ink Monkey waits by a writer as she dips her quill into an ink well. Once the author is done writing the story, the Ink Monkey will

drink whatever ink remains in the well. It was the
simplest creature she could find. It made very little
noise and would take up very little room in her tiny
house on wheels. Her weapon, she decided, would be
a brush that she took from her art box.

She wore her art brush over her left ear and her
one sharp pencil for the year over her right ear. Her
ears were such that they held the instruments quite
well. Along with her Osh-Kosh overalls, she wore a
sweatshirt every day, but upside down and unzipped.
The pockets draped over her bosom while the hood
gave a monkey-like curvature to her butt. She sewed
on it the word SWIMS in large capital letters because
that's the only word she knew that is spelled the same
upside down and backward, much better than a
palindrome.

She didn't want to be a modern comic book
superhero because she felt that Wonder Woman wasn't
ancient enough, had copyright issues, and she couldn't
imagine having to wear itchy leotards to school. Then
there was the problem with plastic pollution.
Superheroes, like Captain Planet, generated tons of
plastics in the form of seldom used toys that grown-ups
buy for children to teach them how to save the planet.
For these reasons, she skipped out on Happy Meals
and forbade anyone from giving her plastic toys while

growing up.

Worst of all, as a superhero, she would eventually have to contend with her foe. The last thing she wanted to see was an Ezequio action figure that would cost her her lunch money and rip her homework in two with its kung fu grip. A part of Wishy-Wishy wished she would never have to deal with Ezequio again. But as the days passed and Ezequio did not lackadaisically answer, "Here" from his empty desk during roll-call, she began to get worried. So too did Mr. Mathis. He asked Wishy-Wishy to stay after class and stepped down from his stool.

"Say, Wishy-Wishy, isn't your father a forest ranger?"

"Why yes, he is," answered Wishy-Wishy.

"I've heard that Ezequio lives deep in the Idlebury Woods. As you can imagine, his absence is of great concern to me. Would you mind asking your father to pick him up tomorrow morning on the way to school? I'd much rather handle this discretely than letting social services get involved."

CHAPTER 6

THE CASTLE

The next morning Mommy Dee fixed up a Canadian breakfast. Wishy-Wishy pulled up the back of her sock and felt the relief of a perfectly flat footbed. There wasn't an itch. She wondered why she hadn't bothered to do this simple thing the morning before while downing a cup of orange juice to wash down her routine poutine. She told Daddy Joe about Ezequio's continuous absence and gave him the address. He put on his ranger hat, and the two made for the Jeep.

They didn't have to drive too far through the backcountry to arrive on a private road. They often looped that way to reach a grocery store, but never bothered to see what lies just beyond the thick thickets. The road stretched half a mile into the woods, where someone went to great lengths to reclaim the land and built a ginormous house that looked like it belonged in Italy. The grass was perfectly manicured and cut short. Putting greens surrounded the east side while earthen berms kept the bayous at bay. It was the kind of house one would expect the CEO of the Cheesecake Factory to own if he had no sense of taste.

It was a Mediterranean villa in the middle of the swamp, and every weathered surface seemed artificially distressed like an attraction at Disneyland. Where no putting greens lie, stood olive trees. Unearned rust and lichen leeched into the stone walls of the mansion.

A woman in her late thirties opened the door.

"What can I do for you today, stranger ranger?"

Daddy Joe took off his hat. "Sorry for the intrusion, but I've been tasked with finding out why..." Daddy Joe searched for the name then looked at Wishy-Wishy.

"Why Ezequio has not shown up to school for five days and counting, not to mention a few other things that I won't mention," said Wishy-Wishy.

"Well right this way then," the lady said and introduced herself as Diane Winterspoon.

Wishy-Wishy felt vertigo when she saw the wagon wheel chandelier hanging from the foyer. Even though the sky outside was infinitely higher, being in such a large open room made her dizzy. She pinched her left earlobe to cope with the nauseating sensation that overtook her. Then came a sense of dread. If she were to play hide and seek in such a place, the seeker would have to call in a search party and a bloodhound. And good luck if the hider happened to cross an indoor water feature.

"Are you Ezequio's mother?" Wishy-Wishy asked.

"Deary me. I get that a lot."

"Is she out of the country or something." Wishy-Wishy said.

Diane sighed then said in a hushed tone, "Ezequio, from what I know, is an orphan." She paused then mentioned, "But don't you ever suggest such a thing to him. He is quite adamant about having had a mother and I suppose everyone at one point or another has had a mother."

"But he mentioned her the other day to me as if he had known her for some time," Wishy-Wishy countered.

"You can't be born out of thin air, right?" Diane replied. "But I am not his mother and neither I or his well-to-do father in absentia of a foster father has ever seen his mother. I am just the estate manager here who happens to care a lot about him." Diane winced for a moment, then went on, "He craves affection so much that he has to make up an imaginary mother."

"How long have you worked here?" Wishy-Wishy

asked.

"Oh for about half a year now. He's hunkered in his room," Diane said pointing off in the distance. "I've tried to coax him out with oatmeal raisin cookies, but he wouldn't budge." She carried a clipboard and checked off a list as she ushered Wishy-Wishy and Daddy Joe along her daily rounds. There was always a toilet that needed flushing or a sink that needed to run for a few seconds. Things went bad when not in use. They made their way down a corridor of candle lit arches then up two flights of stairs toward the end of a loggia. She let Wishy-Wishy flip the switches off and on along the way. It was hard to miss the fallen vases and shredded artwork.

"I do apologize for the mess. He has a habit of leaving a path of destruction. He used a fresco as toilet paper the other day," said Diane.

"He must be going through a rough patch in his life," Wishy-Wishy said. She imagined Ezequio knocking over priceless antiques each time he went to his room and how expensive it must have been to replace the irreplaceable. Did he not appreciate what he had in the slightest? Nestled on what appeared to be a parapet sat Ezequio's room.

"Zeek. You have some friends at the door," Diane announced while knocking.

"Go away. I don't have any friends," Said the voice inside.

After more knocking from Diane, Ezequio finally relented and opened the door.

"Mind if we come in?" Diane asked.

They entered his dimly lit lair. He had drawn down all the shades and only the faintest amount of daylight bled through the edges. He rubbed his brooding eyes. Then he saw her standing there. The girl he tried to shame.

"Oh, it's you," he said to Wishy-Wishy. "What? Did you come back for more insults?"

Wishy-Wishy scowled. "Look. It's not like I want to be here, but Mr. Mathis insisted we check up on you."

"Well, you came, you saw I'm still alive so you can go back home now."

"It's not that simple, Ezequio. Truancy does not look good on your records."

"So now you're a social worker."

Finally, Daddy Joe cut in. "What's keeping you from going to school? You don't look sick."

"When I woke up a few mornings ago…" Ezequio said. He pointed to the glow of the window across the room. They followed him. Then gingerly, he held out his hand and stood to one side while he drew up the shade one click at a time until the tiniest sliver of light pierced through. He held out his pinky finger and then under the direct rays of the sun. It began to smoke. He grimaced, then pulled it out of the light. An acrid smell filled the room and over took the oatmeal raisin cookies. The skin on his finger glowed radicchio red.

"Am I a vampire?" Ezequio asked.

"You don't have any strange craving, do you?" Asked Wishy-Wishy.

Ezequio shook his head. To prove he wasn't a blood-sucking vampire, Diane gave him a bud of garlic and had him nibble on it.

"Seems like an allergic reaction to the sun," said Wishy-Wishy. "Porphyria, to be precise."

"How will I ever go to school again?" Ezequio asked.

It was at that moment Wishy-Wishy had an idea. "Do you have a bucket?" Wishy-Wishy asked Diane.

Diane brought in a red bucket. "The housekeeper normally uses this for the the kitchen floor."

Wishy-Wishy turned to Ezequio and tilted her head slightly.

CHAPTER 7

THE INK MONKEY AND HER SQUONK

"Are we there yet?" Ezequio asked.

Wishy-Wishy led Ezequio through the shady side of the quad to Mr. Mathis' office. They had already missed first period and needed a tardy slip. Ezequio could barely open his eyes, even with sunglasses on. A sloppy coat of mud-covered his hands and face. It was the best sunscreen available. Elephants use it; pigs use it. Wishy-Wishy dipped her art brush into the mud bucket and applied a new layer to Ezequio's face whenever it began to desiccate and shed.

"I've bathed him (in mud), and I've brought him in as you asked, Mr. Mathis," Wishy-Wishy said while lowering the mud bucket with a thud to the floor.

Mr. Mathis gave them a perplexed look. "Well if it isn't the Ink Monkey and her Squonk. The project is not due for another week. For being so late, the two of you managed to turn yourselves in early." He crossed his eyes and shook it off like a dog in rain. "I won't ask how it happened. Let's assume you have come to an arrangement," Mr. Mathis said as if it was common to see a squonk covered in mud from head to toe and an ink monkey liberally applying a fresh coat on his nose.

Mr. Mathis wasn't alone in the room. Lucretia sat on the sofa, waiting for her mother to pick her up. She wore her dark glossy hair in a plain bob-cut. Her wardrobe was often a shimmery sweater and a pair of diamond-patterned jeggings.

Mr. Mathis got down from his stool. "Lucretia, as you may know, was a top student at Mayfair Elementary school last year. But it has come to my attention from Mrs. Figgleworth that Lucretia feels challenged as of late."

"Challenged?" Wishy-Wishy asked.

"Ask her a question she should know, anything."

Wishy-Wishy walked up to Lucretia and asked her to say a word that is spelled the same way upside down and backward.

Lucretia stared blankly into space and moved her mouth like a goldfish gasping for air.

Mr. Mathis sighed. "Somehow, I think this has something to do with you, Wishy-Wishy. Did you by any chance call her something on the first day of school?"

Wishy-Wishy hesitated and then said, "An unwitty

twitty?"

"CHONNNNGG!!!" Mr. Mathis gonged his mouth until his whole body rattled. "And what did you call Ezequio?

"Ezequio Radicchio?"

"DOOOOOHHHHHMMMMM!!!" Mr. Mathis knelled like a death bell.

"Only because they were making fun of my name," Wishy-Wishy added.

"From now on, young woman, you should choose your come-backs wisely."

Mr. Mathis asked Ezequio, "Did you happen to drop by the library as I had suggested?"

The squonk nodded his head.

"What kind of books did you grab?"

"I took a few perma-bounds. And then I ran. I haven't looked at what I swiped. I threw the paper football at the librarian's feet, and then the librarian chased me out the door. It didn't work Mr. Mathis."

"It never does." Mr. Mathis clicked his heels twice then went on, "Now then. Let see about undoing what Wishy-Wishy did to Lucretia. Come to think of it, you can't undo what you did, you can only tweak it just a squeak. I want you, Wishy-Wishy-Woco-Mo-Loco, to close your eyes and think of a different rhyme for Lucretia."

Wishy-Wishy thought long and hard. "Does it have to rhyme, with Lucretia?" Wishy-Wishy asked.

"Okay. Fine. It can be a pun."

Wishy-Wishy thought for a moment longer, but nothing came to mind except "Lucretia of the Black Lagoon."

At that moment, Lucretia snapped back in a British accent. "Girl, you'd bet-uh watch your trap!" She immediately threw her hands over her mouth, surprised at how the words came out. "Why...I sound so sofishycated all of a sud-un. At the same time, I feel like I want to go for a swim. That's it. SWIMS is the word you were thinking, spelled the same way upside down and backward."

"She's back to normal," Wishy-Wishy said.

"A new normal," Mr. Mathis added with an uneasy roll of his eyes.

Lucretia fixed her gaze on the river outside the window in the distance. She licked her dry lips. In an instant, she got up. "Tell my mummy I no longer need of a lift. I shall swim home." With that, she ran to the river. "I'm coming home mummy!" She pinched her nose and hopped right in.

"Should we go after her?" Wishy-Wishy asked.

"She'll be fine. The river is all of two feet deep this time of year," answered Mr. Mathis.

"What just happened?" Ezequio asked.

"It appears every time I resort to name-calling, something weird happens to that person," Wishy-Wishy said.

"Not exactly," Mr. Mathis corrected. "Your name is the trigger word. Whenever you hear your long-form name, and you return with a rhyme or a pun, that's when crazy things happen."

Knowing the plight of so many lesser Gods gripped her with a feeling of sadness. Wishy-Wishy looked at the squonk she created. She was the reason for his condition. And then the words that Bob-Betsy and Bob-Bella chanted rang through her mind.

There's a girl in the world, and she doesn't like her name, what a shame.

Say my name, hear your name, will you ever be the same, say my name.

She begged of him, "If you say my name, maybe I can undo what I did to you. Or at least, turn you into something else."

He didn't say her name.

"Say my name, Ezequio. Make fun of me. I don't want you to stay like this."

"Maybe it's better if I don't," Ezequio said. He

couldn't imagine turning into a worse abomination than what he already was. In a way, he thought he deserved it. He picked up the mud bucket, grabbed an umbrella from the lost and found, it was the only umbrella around, and he said on the way out, "Thank you for the mud. It itches it first, but I think I'm getting used to it."

Kids can be cruel, especially to a mud-covered bully with a yellow umbrella. "They will eat you alive," Wishy-Wishy said. That she could turn him into such a hapless being, it was a power she did not want. For who could ever befriend a squonk?

CHAPTER 8

I NEVER MET A SQUONK THAT FELT SORRY FOR ITSELF

For the next few days, Wishy-Wishy kept a vigil eye on the squonk she created. When it appeared his mud was running low, she would hurl a dollop across the quad, hit him squarely on the face, and spread its soothing properties to grant him instant relief from the sun. "A squonk must be pelted with mud and often by someone who knows how to sling mud," she declared.

Wishy-Wishy had a favorite place to sit during lunch and recess with Adhyaksa. It offered a great birds-eye view of the quad, perfect for student body watching.

To Wishy-Wishy, it just didn't seem right. The quad was missing its usual bully. Without Ezequio to keep the annoying seventh graders in check with his long wingspan, other bullies filled this void in the most unbalanced manner. Whereas Ezequio would only serve up wedgies to boys who were a physical nuisance to other students, these seventh graders now did the same to all incoming sixth graders without much thought. And whereas Ezequio reserved verbal snipes for the smarter students, these seventh graders insulted everyone equally, but their insults lacked specificity and didn't apply to the situation at hand. Wishy-Wishy knew you can't call someone's momma fat when they don't even know you. Would they care if their momma's cell phone number had two zip codes? At least, she thought, these boys won't stoop to Ezequio's level in muddling a girl's yellow dress.

Ezequio meanwhile relegated himself to the dark side of the quad and brooded away on the lawn under his umbrella.

"The nerve of this guy," Wishy-Wishy said. "He has all this money, lives in a ginormous house, and can't be bothered to buy a black umbrella. But, no. He chooses to keep that pansy yellow umbrella that looks more like a parasol from a Monet oil painting. Then he likes to rotate it three times to the left and three times to the right. And what's this? The Squonk can read?"

Ezequio seemed engrossed in the perm-a-bound book he had swiped from the library on the hill.

"I don't understand it myself," said Adhyaksa. She pursed her lips. "He might as well wear white gloves the length of his forearms."

It didn't take long for the band of newly minted seventh-grade bullies to catch on. They detached a mulch bag from a John Deere tractor mower. What was a squonk to do but roll up into a ball to make it oh so easy for them to catch? They reattached the mulch bag back to the tractor mower and gave the quad a fresh trimming. But as they made their way down the fairway, they heard the saddest shrieks and cries come from the bag. It was so loud Mr. Mathis had to cover his ears from his office. It was so sad it reduced everyone to tears, even Jeremy Ledbetter who drove the tractor mower.

When they thought the bag had filled with enough mulch, they all piled on, adding their collective weight.

Wishy-Wishy wasn't going to stand for it. She rolled up her sleeves and made her way down into the quad.

"Well if it isn't Ezequio's girlfriend, Wishywishywocomoloco. What are you going to do about it?"

"Leave him alone Jeremy Ledbetter Bedwetter!" Wishy-Wishy yelled.

"Such big words from a tiny girl."

She tried to pull them off to no avail. She was, after all, a delicate figure.

"Why is he covered in mud. Did he lose a bet?"

"None of your business."

It wasn't until Mr. Mathis showed up with school security that Jeremy stepped aside and went into curious on-looker mode.

Mr. Mathis searched the bag, but all he found was a wet page from Walt Whitman's Leaves of Grass.

When they saw how Ezequio had disappeared, Jeremy and his entourage fled the scene.

"What happened to him?" Wishy-Wishy asked.

"I will miss Ezequio for a few seconds, but not much longer. He has been reduced to tears," Mr. Mathis said. "That's the only way a Squonk can defend itself."

"Should we try to find him?"

"I never met a Squonk that felt sorry for itself," said Mr. Mathis.

"Aren't you going to give Jeremy a detention?"

"None needed. Though you might want to think of a new nickname for Jeremy. No rush."

Wishy-Wishy crossed her eyes inward and slapped her hand on her forehead, realizing what she had done.

The next morning Wishy-Wishy and Adhyaksa saw Ezequio reading his book under his yellow umbrella in the quad as if nothing happened. No one, especially Jeremy Ledbetter, ever bothered him again.

Jeremy had other issues to deal with.

People sometimes drink too much water before going to bed only to have a dream where they need to pee like something fierce. Jeremy found a toilet to relieve himself in his dream. This basin sat on the free-throw line of an NBA basketball court. His mind made up whatever it needed to tell him when it was time. He would have woken up after peeing for five minutes in overtime with thousands of people looking on, only to feel a momentary sense of relief and the need to go again. In this dream, however, he chose to run down the clock and double dribble into triple overtime. By then, it was too late. Game over.

He woke up and changed out of his wet and itchy pajamas, showered, and got ready for school. The next morning, it happened again. He went to bed thirsty the next night to no avail.

CHAPTER 9

COMMAS, DOORS, &
COMMODORE JOE

Wishy-Wishy wondered why she never thought of having a play date before. When the idea came to mind, she used all manners of influence to convince Daddy Joe and Mommy Dee.

"We have to show Adhyaksa how we live," said Wishy-Wishy.

"I don't know," Daddy Joe said. "She might think we're too weird. We might scare her off."

"What if I went over to Adhyaksa's place?"

"I don't believe I've ever had the pleasure of meeting the Narayamamurti family yet.

"But tomorrow's Friday."

"I'm sure they have things to do too."

Mommy Dee would have none of Daddy Joe's nonsense.

"Wishy-Wishy. You can have a play date, but we have rules in this house. You have to be home by 4:30."

"But we get out at 3:15. And it may take 30 minutes to make it to Adhy's house," Wishy-Wishy complained.

"Space and time are entirely different yet one and the same. What do we say in this family?"

"It's not the amount of space, it's the quality of time spent within that space. It's not the amount of time, it's the quality of the space within that time."

"And if you had to cover too much space?"

"I won't have time."

"Good. Now I'll have to square this away with Adhyaksa's parents when I get a chance tomorrow."

Wishy-Wishy gave Mommy Dee her friend's home phone number and went straight to her room.

She told Adhyaksa the good and the bad. The two spent the day devising how they could maximize their playtime with only half an hour to play. At lunch, Adhyaksa described her living situation to Wishy-Wishy. She wanted to get all the unnecessary details and introductions out of the way.

"I live in a bungalow. 454 Obsidian View. Southside of Mayfield County. I share a room with my host sister in the attic. It's a shared space. So I will not call it my room. It's not like I had my own room in India. Back home, I share a room with my two sisters."

"So you're a foreign exchange student."

"Yes, in case you couldn't tell how lost I get when Mr. Mathis tells his math jokes."

"Amazing."

"What about you, Wishy-Wishy?"

"I live in a bus, a double-decker bus, like the kind you would find in England."

Adhyaksa's face lit up. "That is so cool!"

"I don't know how my Daddy Joe got his hands on one, but it has been our home as of late. But I'm not as lucky as you, Adhy. I wish I had a sibling to play with. Sometimes, often times, I get lonely."

"You're trying to tell me you're normal?"

"Yes. Dreadfully normal."

"Then you can be my sister too, Wishy-Wishy."

They made a pact to share their deepest secrets.

"Why do you rhyme so much when you get excited?" Adhyaksa asked.

"It's more like a reflex, a nervous tick. All the poems Mr. Mathis reads to start out a class? They may be things I've never read, things I've yet to understand, but I already know them. I know them by heart and I don't know why."

"I wish I was a native speaker, like you."

"It's overrated. I wouldn't last a second on the Indian Subcontinent, which makes me wonder. Didn't the British colonize India?"

"Yes, but India is a big country. Many dialects and different castes." Adhyaksa let out a simpering sigh. "My family is anything but royalty. And my school in Hyderabad is tech-centric." She smiled, then went on, "all into computer and coding. They did not teach much grammar. It's something they gloss over and expect us to know. For example, how do you know where to place a comma or a semicolon in a sentence? I've tried it with dictation software, and there was a pain in the colon."

"It's easy. You do it all the time. Breathe in. Breathe out." Wishy-Wishy took a deep breath, held it for a while, then slowly let it out. "Now you do it."

As Adhyaksa drew her breath and released it, Wishy-Wishy explained, "Grammar has more to do with breathing in and out than any hard fast rules. The next time you want to write a sentence that flows, I want you to breathe in, then breathe out."

"That's it?"

"That's it. It's a useful useless thing Grammarian Joe taught me at a very young age. And when it comes to comma placement, all you need to do is say it in your mind. And when you pause to take a breath, you can smile for a comma. If you feel you need to hold your breath; purse your lips before saying something just as important and it's a semicolon."

For the rest of the school day, Adhyaksa smiled where the commas would fall and pursed her lips whenever the sentence she wrote called for a semicolon. No one knew what she was doing except for Wishy-Wishy. She found Adhyaksa absolutely adorable with her purple crayon. She wanted to bottle that moment forever but forever meant there wouldn't have been time for a play date.

Wishy-Wishy met Adhyaksa after school and walked rather slow for someone who had to make the most of time. What could she do with so little time before she had to be home?

"Why so sad, Wishy-Wishy?"

"I don't know what we could possibly do with only half an hour to spare. I have to be home by 4:30."

Adhyaksa let out a chuckle. "Your parents didn't tell you?"

"Tell me what?"

A foghorn broke the silence. Into the bus loop wheeled Wishy-Wishy's double-decker home. It was a spectacle to behold. When she had to be home, home came to her. That meant the limits of time had been lifted for the day. And it seemed as if Adhyaksa was doing the inviting.

"C'mon, let's check out your house on wheels."

Adhyaksa took Wishy-Wishy by the hand and pulled her along. Wishy-Wishy was both thrilled and apprehensive.

"Why don't you give me a tour of my own home while you're at it."

"Don't mind if I do," said Adhyaksa, pretending to be familiar with the layout of the house. They couldn't just barge right in. It was an English house on wheels which meant they had to enter from the other side of the bus because there was a time when it drove on the left side of the road. The accordion doors opened and closed a few times before opening for good and actually played accordion music while doing so. "Right up the steps, the first thing we see is a toilet with steering wheels?"

"It's a 1.5 bathroom house," said Wishy-Wishy. "Brown on top, deep blue on the bottom. Sometimes it reminds me of a floating log over the swirling seas. Sometimes Daddy Joe needs to strap himself in before going on a wild ride." The engine hummed with a cyclic rumble. Wishy-Wishy rolled her eyes and went on:

Ode to my abode above the commode
There's a price I pay to see the open road
for a certain miasma could trigger my asthma

62

❊ ❊ ❊

O when the seas get rough
and there's trouble down below
And enough is enough
and the fog horn blows
Who could it be?

Commodore Joe…

He will strap himself in
For a wild, wild ride
He will grip the wheels tight
with all his might
before closing eyes
Who could it be?

Commodore Joe…

For when you're stuck in a rut
no need to hold it in your gut
no need to take it on the go
just let it flow
like Commodore Joe

Commodore Joe…

❊ ❊ ❊

So let the news hit the fan
with a flash in the pan
don't forget to wash your hands,
you can smile once again
my Commodore Joe

Commodore Joe…

Because a certain miasma
could trigger my asthma
O would you, could you
not open the commode door?
Commodore Joe?

Commodore Joe…

In the event you need to vent
you can vent to the side
Just try to spare the gents
who walk on by
you Commodore Joe

Commodore Joe…

You can press harder the retarder
You can slow things down

You can crank up the fan
Blow it out the door and into town
Let your foghorn go like Commodore Joe

Commodore Joe! {all together}

{Fog horn blows.}

Other than that, the house was an ordinary tiny house on wheels, except for the firemen's pole from Wishy-Wishy's reading nook to the floor below, and not to mention the cargo net that made up the floor of the floating nook and spanned the area above the lounge.

Wishy-Wishy climbed up the stairs, threw her self onto the cargo net and invited Adhyaksa to do the same. "Try it. It's fun." The two pretended they had showered in pixie dust. They stretched out their arms, and when they looked to the side and out the windows, it seemed as they were flying above the road and among the clouds while the house cruised down the highway.

They took a break from flying and looked up through the skylight above. Mommy Dee handed them a bowl of Moondrop grapes from below. From what Adhyaksa could see, everything about Wishy-Wishy's room was fun and cheerful, except for the most dreadful pair of lamps that didn't seem to belong. They had floral wooden spirals on either side and the shades were rather ornate with their streaks of gold leafs.

"Oh. Those guys," Wishy-Wishy said. "We got them from a consignment store after they sat there for half a year and no one bought them. The previous owners had to sell them because they were Baroque."

Adhyaksa felt compelled to ask Wishy-Wishy a few questions based on her observations, from what she had seen during the first few weeks of school.

She asked, "Why is it that we are required to get a C in Mr. Mathis' English class?"

"I'm not so sure I know," Wishy-Wishy answered.

"It's just that in Hyderabad, we are always encouraged to do our best. It doesn't make any sense why they do things this way in your country."

"I've not given it much thought. I was homeschooled until late last year, so I'm not sure how things are supposed to be. But I can tell you it takes more effort to get a perfect C than it does to get a perfect A. You have to know all the right answers, so that you can correctly choose 3 out of ten wrong answers."

"But here's the thing. I don't know about me, but every kid in Mr. Mathis' class has a special ability. They may not test well in every subject, but they can hold their own in their area of specialty.

"Like an idiot savant?"

"More than that. Do you have a computer?"

"Let me get out my bike."

"What does biking have to do with a computer?"

Wishy-Wishy pulled a lever on the wall and lowered a bicycle from the ceiling. The floorboards separated to reveal a pair of metal rolling pins. It was a dynamo that supplied power for a laptop she mounted on the bike. She had unlimited screen time in her house. The only catch was she had to supply the power herself. The later in the day it got, the more rolling resistance the rolling pins provided. When the bike wasn't mounted to the generator, she liked to go riding with Selfie Alfie, her pet rooster whose job it was to keep a tiny video camera on his head which acted like a gimbal no matter how much the road rattled and dipped.

While Wishy-Wishy pedaled, Adhyaksa brought up a terminal prompt and typed in some cryptic commands. She brought up another window that was like a secret back door to the world.

"You'd be surprised how much you can find out

about a kid by looking at what their parents post on social media," Adhyaksa said. "Take Sean Karcher for instance. You wouldn't know by looking at him that he is gifted with string instruments. Imagine how wonderful it would be if we could hear him play the violin when we happen to walk past a rehearsal in music class. And then there's Samantha Fontaine. She can sprint faster than anyone in school. And Zepherine Jones? He can deadlift 500 pounds. And before she jumped into the river and left the school district, Lucretia Chen was a gifted swimmer."

"Did you make any other observations?"

"I looked into Jeremy Bedwetter — I mean Ledbetter. Jeremy hasn't managed a letter grade since kindergarten."

"They don't give out letter grades in kindergarten."

"My point exactly. Yet somehow he is still able to matriculate year after year and lo, he's in seventh grade and still picking on other kids. So I searched even deeper and found out that he's the son of the governor."

"That explains it. How do you know all these things?"

"I peeked into some records. School. City. State."

"Peeked?"

"Okay. I spoofed and I hacked." Adhyaksa let out

a cough and quickly changed the subject. "Which brings me to you. You were homeschooled so there's hardly anything on you, except for the time you placed second place in the school spelling bee."

"Oh. That. I'd rather not talk about it. I would have won if it wasn't for Ezequio."

"What did he do? Win?"

"No. Someone else must have won, but I don't remember."

"What is it with you and Ezequio? For someone who finds him annoying, you sure do follow him around school a lot. Almost like you're spying on him. Do you by any chance like him?"

"You are quite the interloper." Wishy-Wishy twiddled her little thumbs and whittled a brittle answer. "But you're right. It's kind of strange. He may act all tough on the outside, but on the inside, he's a wimp. I can't help but feel responsible for turning him into a squonk. It's like I turned him inside out for the world to see."

"What's a squonk?"

"A squonk is the saddest, most pathetic mythological creature on the planet. Such a creature can only originate on American soil, and I will not say which parts. His ginormous home is a vapid wasteland, devoid of any meaningful discourse. Those terrible cries you heard in the quad were his only defense when Jeremy Ledbetter and his gang attacked him."

"I couldn't help but cry as well when I heard it," said Adhyaksa.

"The only use you could have for a squonk is for him to cry out for help in battle. But by the time you hear his wailing, you might as well walk the other way for the battle is already lost. That's the conventional wisdom, anyway."

Wishy-Wishy reached through the net and grabbed a Patrick O'Brien novel from a built-in shelf below. "Commodore Joe tells me that in victory, you must be responsible for the defeated. I may not like Ezequio, but I bear a burden for the squonk I created. He is my squonk to care and look after. But don't let his condition fool you. He can still be a jerk."

"Is that so?" There were a few other people she looked up, but Adhyaksa wanted Wishy-Wishy to find out for herself.

CHAPTER 10

THE CAMPUS ON A HILL

One morning, Adhyaksa had to return a book to the library on the hill. She was close to finishing it and didn't want to bother renewing, so she read the remaining few pages as she hiked up the hill. By the time George had finished giving Lenny a final pep talk in *of Mice and Men*, Adhyaksa had wandered far beyond the path Mr. Mathis had told her not to stray. She looked over the ridge and saw a vast open plain. She imagined Neoclassical lecture halls and a brick-laden causeway. At the center stood a water fountain and an obelisk because why not?

She mustn't let her imagination run away, she thought. She dreamed of attending such a learning institution in a few years. Maybe not this one, but one that looked just like it in Boston or nestled away in the hills of Los Angeles. Or maybe she would rub elbows with some Bollywood stars in Mumbai.

To attend a learning institution like this, she would need better than perfect grades, even if she was just a foreign exchange student. It had to start early, at a young age. She was self-motivated. And then Adhyaksa got curious. What would happen if she scored 100% on everything? She had already aced her pre-Algebra quarter-end tests. The only thing holding her back from straight A's was Mr. Mathis' English class. She remembered what Mr. Mathis had warned. Do too well, and she will move to a normal English class. And what was wrong with that? She would miss having Wishy-Wishy in class. But she could just as easily convince Wishy-Wishy to ace all her assessment test so that she too could advance. On the other hand, she knew that Wishy-Wishy loved Mr. Mathis' class and could care less about grades.

At home, Adhyaksa studied the grammar book Wishy-Wishy had given her after their play date. It wasn't long before she learned the difference between the articles "a" and "the." It turned out that if a subject has not been introduced in conversation, she should use "a." On the other hand, if something was already mentioned and she needed to refer to it again, then she should use "the." She soon moved on to gerunds, appositives, noun clauses, and predicate nominatives. She applied the same patient method Wishy-Wishy taught her when she needed to master the placement of commas and semicolons. Just as Wishy-Wishy had explained, punctuations and the flow of sentences had more to do with breathing than it did with hard fast rules. People could only say so much in one breath before they need to pause. This pausing to take a breath translated to the written world in the form of punctuations and clauses. When she fragmented her sentences, she wasn't exhaling enough before drawing her next breath. Too much of this could lead to hyper-ventilation.

Adhyaksa fidgeted with her mechanical pencil a few times. She knew it was contraband, but how was she supposed to get good grades if she didn't equip her self with sharp writing utensils? She had four different kinds of mechanical pencils at her disposal. For bubbling in multiple choice answers, she used her shaker mechanical pencil to save her precious seconds she would lose from having to advance the lead with her thumb. A simple shake of the wrist did the trick. For general doodling during a boring lecture, she resorted to her German-engineered, brass-bodied rOtring mechanical pencil with 2mm lead. If the lecture got interesting, and she found it hard to keep up, she would switch to a Japanese pencil with a special cushioning mechanism to keep the lead from breaking. But when she needed the 0.5 mm lead to stay sharp, she deployed her Uni Kuru Toga mechanical pencil with an auto-rotating tip that "self-sharpened" with every press.

When Adhyaksa calmed her breathing, she found out she could write the most mellifluous sentences. She also noticed that as listeners, people only had so much mental breath they could use to repeat what they had heard. She realized that the people who wrote run-on sentences also spoke in run-on sentences. They never took the time to breathe in and out to collect their thoughts into a clear message. They often polluted their speech with the word "like" when they didn't really like what they were talking about.

Once Adhyaksa made up her mind on getting good grades, nothing could stop her.

CHAPTER 11

PICTURE DAY

Lewis Middle School was not always a middle school. In its former incarnation, it was a high school. But over time, perhaps due to people having fewer children, the school shrunk into a middle school. Before it was a high school, it was a homestead settlement, a historical landmark until the city decided it was better to use the houses as classrooms. It had a nondenominational church building with a bell tower, perfect for letting kids know when it was time to return from recess.

The end of the first quarter was also picture-day. This was the time when Lewis Middle School saw, or rather, never saw a visitor from the forgotten campus to the north. To describe what he looked like would be total nonsense for he was rarely ever seen. But if he were to be seen, he would have had furry claws, eyes of flame, rubbery wings, and a mouth that loved to sputter utter nonsense most of the time. He would have worn a red vest, perhaps a throwback to the time when he cared about keeping up appearances. But who needs appearance? When you're a Jabberwock, you can freeze time. He traveled with a cadre of three assistants. They made their way to the GATE cluster, a building behind some white gates where the great young minds of Lewis Middle School had coalesced. It was more of a hen house where all the students had been unknowingly tested and presorted for easy Jabberwock consumption.

"Snot drops on noses and flea-bitten kittens, these are a few of my favorite things." The Jabberwock picked a flower and sniffed the life out of it. "Come along, my colleagues. It is time for the culling."

His cadre consisted of three Nordic mental fitness trainers. Their jobs: to help assess the mental fitness of prospective students and encourage the ones who nearly made the cut. One of the trainers had muscular hands which you wouldn't want to play mercy with. His specialty was thumb wrestling Icelandic supermodels, but most of the time he was a one-dimensional multi-tool or just a plain tool to deal with. The second one wielded an ax of sorts and everywhere he went he lugged his clumsy grindstone. He had the nasty habit of spitting into his hands before shaking other people's hands. He always had an ax to grind. The third mental fitness trainer had a set of redundant wings behind her ears to go with the ones behind her back. She wore blue armor, was rather pretty and seemed to be around more for motivational purposes.

Then with a snap, the Jabberwock said, "Nick-Knack-Patty-Wack."

The classroom full of gifted students who tested well came to a standstill. The Jabberwock goose-stepped to the first frozen child he saw. The child had raised his hands. There was an eager expression on his face that said *pick me, pick me. I know the answer.*

"There's nothing I love more than a young child's mind. So hopeful. So creative. So full of imagination." The Jabberwock spread his warbled hands, placed it over Adrian Winklewort's head, and read what this beautiful mind had to offer. But instead of Isaac Newton or Mozart, all the Jabberwock could see were Adrian's hands holding a package. And all he could hear was Adrian's squeaky voice inside a hollow room saying, "Hey guys! Welcome to Adrian's secret toy unboxing. Today we'll be taking the wraps off an awesome Nina the Ninja action figure. Oops, did I just reveal what I'm about to unwrap?" The scene was poorly lit with a dim-watt bulb and had little to no production value.

"Must be a fluke," said the Jabberwock. He scanned further into the future, but all he saw was the bottom half of Adrian's face with glittering lip gloss. And all he could hear was Adrian whispering, "Hey guys. Today I will eat something crunchy," followed by the sound of teeth mashing down on celery sticks and the gulping sound of aloe Vera."

The Jabberwock groaned with disappointment. He straightened out Adrian's collar and neatened up his hair. "Moving on then."

Sparing everyone the repeated dramatics, he ordered his minions to line up the GATE cluster for him to scan en mass. The Jabberwock flapped his stretchy wings and hovered above. He sent warbly sonic waves all around. They bounced off ear drums, cleared out Eustachian tubes, loosened parmesan tonsiliths, shadowboxed uvulas and tintinaubulated throughout the room and out the door. But just when he was about to read everyone's minds, he sensed something. Struggle. Victory. Greatness. It did not come from within that room, but elsewhere in the distance across the quad.

"Send them to the queue and update the yearbook records. I will deal with them later."

"Yes, my lord." Answered his three Nordic mental fitness trainers. The Jabberwock had only enough energy to do one mass scan per year and a few suspensions of time and disbelief. He left much of the daily heavy lifting to his loyal and trusting minions who curried his favor with hopes of reliving glorious dreams of yore.

Meanwhile, in room 53, Wishy-Wishy tussled with her squonk over a manila envelope.

"Give it back to her now, you filthy squonk."

Wishy-Wishy launched herself off Caoimhe Bittinheigh's desk. She tackled her squonk to the ground, scraped off a layer of mud and made him buck and whine and squeal like a swine and crawl on hands and knees. He recoiled into the dark corner of the room, dragging her along. She pinned him down on his back, straddled herself across his chest, grabbed him by his flannel collar and said, "If you can't stand your miserable self then don't take it out on my friend. There's only one way we can fix this, but you gotta work with me here. Say.. my.. name."

He wouldn't say it.

"You know what? I'm going to tell on you. Who's your daddy?"

Silence.

"SAY MY NAME! WHO'S YOUR DADDY? SAY MY NAME! WHO'S YOUR DADDY?"

She wanted to slap him, but realized it would have been a breach of social etiquette.

He could have easily tossed this Ink Monkey far

into the center of the quad, but he couldn't bear the sound of broken glass. "Very well," he said and relinquished his grip on the envelope. She left him there and with the goods, she came galumphing back.

"Here Adhyaksa. Your report card. You may open it now." Wishy-Wishy blew her bangs out of her eyes, fixed the murf on her turf, and returned to her seat. "O Frabjous Day! Callooh! Callay!" She chortled in her joy, and kicked the red mud bucket in her squonk's general direction.

Adhyaksa stared at her test results. She couldn't believe her eyes. She got every grammar question correct. Her shorthand sentences were perfect and meaningful. They were a delight to read in her mind and in Mr. Mathis'. The comments in tiny and barely perceptible letters read, "You have a mastery of the written world." Having read these words, Adhyaksa felt a great sense of accomplishment. She achieved her straight A's for the quarter, had perfect attendance, and made a friend for the rest of her life, her triple crown.

Wishy-Wishy turned to her squonk and shouted, "Stop being such a wet blank…" -She became frozen in time.

The Jabberwock's spell caught everyone *en media res*. Mr. Mathis was about to sink his teeth into his favorite chocolate peanut butter cup. Wishy-Wishy paused in mid-speech, her mouth, slurring a contorted word that didn't make for an intelligent demeanor. She wore a disheveled hairdo. Mud prints stained her dress. Her mind was in mid-thought, so her eyes rolled up into their sockets. When the Jabberwock looked more carefully, a line of saliva ran from her canine tooth to her bicuspid. He slid the tip of his terribly sharp claw between her top incisors, removed a stubborn piece of parsley from the night before, and flicked it into the air. Not only did Wishy-Wishy not test well, she often did not photograph well either.

The Jabberwock turned to his left and gawked at the most horrendous thing, a boy bathed in mud. Yes, this had to be the bottom of the barrel. Then at the head of the class, he couldn't believe what he saw. A former demon slayer, Mr. Mathis, was reduced to teaching below basic English to this group of dullards. And even though he saw the words Synecdoche and Metonymy scrawled on the board, the Jabberwock didn't make much of it. How could these sieves possibly absorb what Mr. Mathis was trying to teach? After all, "An old fart does not hold fast to dry sponge." He took what he saw in Wishy-Wishy and Ezequio to represent the whole.

"But I sensed greatness," he muttered to himself.

Then he saw her. Adhyaksa sat upright with

perfect posture gazing far into her future. The Jabberwock came to collect what he thought would be an ordinary extraordinary prize. But when he read her mind, it sent goose egg goosebumps down his spine.

"Her penmanship is mere chicken scratch, and I can't read what she wrote with these blasted crayons. But who would have thought a remedial English class could have such a brilliant child? — A diamond in the rough. What imagery, what lore — I absolutely adore. What passion, what legend, I do implore. Show me more!"

Adhyaksa came from India. And in her mind, the Jabberwock saw slithering races of serpentine beings, soft-spoken angels with broken dreams, and blue-tinged fallen gods of cosmic descent. There was such a rich new complexity in these characters.

At once, he had grown weary of his Nordic mental fitness trainers and his Nordic Track skier exercise thingamajig, anything Nordic in general. The Nordic track record was spotty at best, and he had let things slide for the longest time. It was a stretch trying to get them to do the simplest things. They may have brought about the financial ruin and political instability he so desperately craved, but they wanted flexible work hours, six weeks of paid vacation, and didn't deliver on the sculpted abs they promised. It was a clumsy affair. There were always strings attached, an internal struggle, an existential give and take. He could feel the tension ratcheting up on either side, yet his arms still sagged. He had greased the wheels long enough. "Time for a new regiment."

"Haven't we but served you, my lord?"

"Some things just don't work-out," said the Jabberwock.

In their place arose the three new Mental Fitness Devas: a three-headed serpent Naga Prince, an Apsara Queen with dripping wings, and a Lapiz Lazuli encrusted Asura Devil who had fallen from Mount Meru a long, long time ago. It was said that Naga Kings often had seven slithering heads, but this one only had three. It was said that all the apsaras that lined the temple walls of Angkor Wat wore a beaming smile, but this Apsara Queen wore a frown. It was said that the Asuras once flourished in the upper echelons of Mount Meru, but this blue devil fell far from grace and was banished by Vishnu himself. These were the new beings who would help the Jabberwock rule his new dominion.

"Serve my deeds and I will restore you to your former glory," declared the Jabberwock. He lifted Adhyaksa with care and handed her off to the serpent Naga Prince.

"So meaningful, the dreamer of my dreams. She is perfect in every way," said the Jabberwock. "Promote her to top of the feed."

"What's that?" The blue devil asked.

"Training on flow charts and proper procedures, laws, and by-laws, social networks, and non-edible and difficult to digest torts of many sorts will commence at 3 am," said the Jabberwock.

On the way out, the Jabberwock took the opportunity to gloat in resonant demonic tone.

"Thought you had slain me with your terrible math jokes, did you, little boy Roy? Or shall I say Roy Math-is-not? You might have struck me down with your vorpal blade, but I was always around, lurking in the fine print of that economy car you leased, hiding in synergy and best practices of the business writing classes you had to take to become a principal, lingering in a litany of subscriptions you never bothered to cancel or the penny principle on a student loan you forgot to kill. Interest accrues behind your ecru colored eyes and your day of reckoning will soon be at hand. Just when you think you've climbed out, you dig yourself a deeper hole. You've been living on borrowed time. But this is a non-conventional loan. As interest grows, this principal shrinks, and terrible math jokes don't help either."

Just to make sure he left Mr. Mathis with a bad taste in his mouth, the Jabberwock replaced Mr. Mathis' favorite chocolate peanut butter cup with some rhesus feces. He also reached into Mr. Mathis' sack and replaced his hair gel with a new shellac made from the hacking cough of a black macaque. Then with a nick-nack-patty-wack, the Jabberwock and his newly minted minions vanished.

"...ket," said Wishy-Wishy while losing her train of thought. She saw the mud on her clothes and didn't know how they got that way.

Mr. Mathis woke from the Wock's not so woke trance and chewed thoughtfully before spitting out the vile and nutty-bitter candy he thought was well past its expiration date. He felt something like a low-blow gut punch, but he couldn't pinpoint where it had come from. He reached for his Tum-Tum tree, popped some antacids in his mouth, but it only added to the swirling mystery.

Nobody knew the Jabberwock was ever there. It was his greatest trick. Gone too was Adhyaksa. No one knew she was ever around. No one knew she ever existed, not even Wishy-Wishy.

English class went on as usual. Mr. Mathis shook his eyes back into place and resumed his lecture on synecdoche and metonymy. Needless to say, all eyes were on Mr. Mathis and Wishy-Wishy was all ears. It was at that moment that Wishy-Wishy looked down and realized how small Mr. Mathis' shoes had become. She didn't realize it before. It must have happened so gradually that she could not perceive the difference on a day to day basis.

As if asking Mr. Mathis a totally unrelated question to the topic at hand, Wishy-Wishy said, "Why are your shoes so small?"

"You're right, Wishy-Wishy, they look like a pair of kitten mittens." The realization came in little oodles, then grew into the whole kit and kaboodle.

"Why are you the size of Heathcliff the cat?" Wishy-Wishy asked.

It startled the class. Ezequio jumped out of his seat and squatted on his desk as the classroom filled with careless whispers among good friends.

"Oh don't mind my condition," Mr. Mathis said, trying to settle the class down. "I have JDD. Jocular Degenerative Disease. I must have contracted it while getting my juris doctorate degree. It affects one in 8 billion people. Nothing to be ashamed of and it's not contagious. I haven't been able to isolate the cause. Though I have been able to replicate the symptom to great effect."

"That's no small task. But what exactly is JDD?"

Zepherine asked.

"Actually, it is a small task." Mr. Mathis corrected. "Every time I tell a joke, I shrink. -Definitely, if it's a bad math joke and especially if the joke falls flat, doesn't connect, needs a diagram, or worse, is corrected by an astute listener who steals my thunder." He looked squarely at Wishy-Wishy.

"That sounds serious," Wishy-Wishy said. "English teachers should not be telling math jokes, good or bad. Why didn't you tell us about this earlier?"

Mr. Mathis looked at the ceiling, then the floor. "That's exactly what I was trying to do. I wanted to see how well you grasshoppers pay attention -and note my use of metonymy. I've been dishing out one bad math joke after another for weeks now and no one took note of my shrinkage?" His eyes crossed. "Let me throw some cold water on it and walk that one back. You were supposed to ask 'Why are you three inches shorter?' -Not wait until I'm the size of a pussy cat."

"See something, say something," said the squonk.

"Yes. You were supposed to take pity on me and pamper me. 'Can I get that for you, Mr. Mathis? How's the weather down there, Mr. Mathis? Pardon my britches, Mr. Mathis. Looks like you could sure use a pick-me-up, Mr. Mathis.' If you want, I can tell you another math joke…" The class looked at random things and avoided eye contact.

"Please don't," Wishy-Wishy said. "I'm sorry I didn't give it the attention it deserved. I noticed it earlier, but I didn't want to bring it up because I thought it might embarrass you or that you might be mad at me for not noticing it sooner. But then you got smaller and smaller. And some days, I forgot to remind myself. Sometimes I just want to sweep you under a rug. And then I saw your shoes today and it seemed like the oddest thing in the world."

Mr. Mathis let out a sigh of acceptance. "I suppose ADD will always win out over JDD."

"How far along is the disease?" Wishy-Wishy asked.

"At least someone is anxiously listening. I'm at stage 6.6 JDD. The disease is measured as a ratio of my original height of 2.2 meters divided by my current height. But enough about me. Let's start on the next book I want you guys to read. Now that we have completed *Wuthering Heights*, which was probably a tad too complicated for our grade level, let's dial it back down to something we can all be more comfortable with. *Little Women*."

It was only then that the class noticed a ladder

running up and down the stool he sat on every day.

CHAPTER 12

MINGLING WITH MACADAMIA

What was she going to say to Daddy Joe and Mommy Dee? Mr. Mathis has shrunk to the size of a cat? She got into a wrestling match with a squonk? It would have explained the mud. This will have been the fifth set of clothes she soiled this year. It didn't help that it happened on picture day. Any mention of shrinkage or squonk would have resulted in Mommy Dee saying, "You have such an overactive imagination, young lady." And perhaps Daddy Joe would dredge up from the swamps an old nickname and say, "Silly The Chubican."

Chubican was not a political party that quarreled with Chubicats and loved to munch on mugwumps (otherwise known as Rechubicans), but a nickname Daddy Joe gave her when she was a toddler. The proper way to say it was "The Chubican," so technically, her first name was "The" and sometimes

Daddy would only call her "The" and reserve her full name for when he wanted The Chubican to clean her chubby room.

The Chubican was not born. She was hatched. The Chubican's natural habitat was Daddy Joe's left foot. She wrapped herself around his leg and clung to it like a sack of potatoes. The Chubican could read before she could walk, could multiply before she could count. The Chubican knew so many words that Daddy Joe needed to refer to everything as chubby to keep things simple.

Before she was an Ink Monkey, Wishy-Wishy rationalized, she was Jane, and before that, she was The Chubican.

But she was fast becoming a young woman, and The Chubican's chubby cheeks had long ago faded. Her clothes started to fit differently. It didn't matter all that much when she soiled an outfit she would only outgrow.

On a cloudy weekend, she happened to look out the window while cruising to the spa with Mommy Dee. A young Spanish boy about her age jogged along the side of the road and quickly faded into the rearview mirror. He had such a carefree stride and seemed to float across the land.

By the time he caught up to the roadside spa,

Wishy-Wishy had already had a mud mask placed on her face. She loved mud masks. She didn't mind it at all when Ezequio smeared mud on her cheek. It always starts cold. But if you give it warmth, you can make it your own.

While Daddy Joe might have taught Wishy-Wishy useful useless things that often amounted to the regurgitation of some factoid, Mommy Dee took a different approach with her daughter. She often took Wishy-Wishy on weekend excursions to teach her the fine art of public speaking. When you're born speaking properly, the only thing left to learn is how to speak improperly. Wishy-Wishy had done her rendition of a valley girl and even dabbled in a little Eliza Doolittle or had been faschizzeled from time to time. Today was a special treat for something special showed up.

She saw the Spanish boy through the glass door in the lobby. He took a seat and reached into his tote bag and took out a bento box of mixed spring vegetables, drizzled on some EVOO and balsamic vinegar, and went over it with a mini peppercorn grinder and a pinky pink pinch of Himalayan rock salt. He uncapped a paring knife and peeled half an apple before slicing it into the salad. He gave it a light toss then took in the aroma, savored the moment. They say digestion starts with the nose. He licked his upper lip and wore a patient gentle smile.

But he did not eat the salad. He put it away and instead bit into the remaining half of the apple. It happened rather quickly. Even though a glass door divided them, she could hear the rupture of pink lady apple skin, feel the juices hit her mouth, taste the sweet tartness such fruit would impart on her salivating tongue. She gripped the corner of her chair. Her eyes roamed into their upper limits.

That apple…So mouth-watering. Where did he get it? Should I retrieve the seeds from the core and ask Daddy Joe to plant it? Would it produce the same fruit like the apple it came from?

Alas, she came to the realization that even if she planted the seeds, it would not guarantee the apple would look the same, crunch the same or taste the same. If she wanted the fruit of knowledge, she would need to rip up the tree of knowledge from the ground and make it her own. "Apples come from the same varietal. Once you find an apple tree you like, you take its branches and you graft it to another tree. You can trace any apple varietal to the same tree," Botanist Joe used to say. Wishy-Wishy realized there was nothing special about this apple. All she would need to do was pick up the Tuesday mailers and look for loss-leading pink lady apples on sale for a dollar a pound. She regained her composure.

The boy reached for the water dispenser, but only to find it was empty. He had to come inside for a refill.

With Mommy Dee fast asleep, Wishy-Wishy said to the boy in her best Southern drawl, "Noticed you trott'n along back yonder. Are ya new to these parts?" The lime-green mud mask she wore allowed her to talk however she wanted.

The boy took off his wireless earbuds and ran his fingers through a mane of golden hair. There was a sense of sophisticated simplicity in his *joie de vivre* like he could turn the act of nose picking into a special occasion with the right set of tools.

"I'm sorry. I was listening to some Brazilian Bossanova," he said.

She was expecting death metal. He wore an onion skin Patagonia windbreaker and there was something provincial, yet suave about the way he spoke, a Catalonian accent if she had ever heard one. -And who runs while listening to Bossanova music anyway? He spoke with a slight lisp. It must have been due to the retainers he wore on his upper teeth.

"I says ya new to them here parts?" Wishy-Wishy repeated.

"Don't mind me. I'm just out for a pleasure run."

"Pleasure run?"

"It's something I treasure, a run, at my own leisure, for pleasure."

"I'm gonna have to add that to my ledger." She took the pencil she wore on her ear and licked it sharp because sharpening was not allowed. Then she jotted down on her pocket notebook a series of lines and dots. She had never heard the two words used in the same sentence or juxtaposed in such a way, why with her asthma inhaler and all. His skin was so clear. He hadn't broken out in a sweat. It was like an oxymoron without any zits.

"I reckon I might could go for one of them there pleasure runs if I weren't strapped to this doggone gurney," she said.

"I am Francisco Roberto Romero. But I normally go by my middle name."

"Roberto then?"

"Si. Et tu?"

"My name is Alejandra, but don't call my name, Roberto."

He let out a chuckle. "Mind if I join you?"

"Not at all. Make yureself comfy," she said, biting her lip for she never thought she would have to keep up a phony southern drawl for more than a few sentences.

He eased himself into his massage recliner. "I won't call your name. I hope you don't find this weird, but this is what Catalonian boys often do on a pleasure run. This is the most rewarding part of a pleasure run.

"A massage?"

"And a skin peel. A time for me to sit back and reflect. It's how I grow."

"Of course, of course. -I never knew that. And thank you."

And who was she to question? And why would a young boy with perfect skin need a skin peel? With the notepad and pencil, Wishy-Wishy looked like a non-judgmental shrink. It didn't take long for Roberto to unravel.

"I have two brothers. We are identical triplets, although we don't really look alike. My eldest brother is Roberto Francisco Romero, so he goes by?"

"Romano?"

"No. Romano is a type of cheese. His middle name is Francisco so, like me, he goes by Francisco."

"Oh yes, yes. Francisco..Francisco..Francisco…"

"And my younger brother goes by Romero so his name is?"

"Francisco Bolero Roberto?"

"No. Bolero is a music composition."

"Right you are." She gave him a military salute.

"By the way. I'm Cleo."

"That's easy to remember."

This thirteen-year-old boy wore something to hide a certain smell, but Wishy-Wishy couldn't place it. It was so thick she thought she could take an axe to it.

"Tell me, Francisco Roberto Romero. What else do boys your age do to shoot the breeze in Catalonia?"

"Shoot the breeze?"

"Dew for faun," she said while giving her gooey Japanese natto a good stir with a pair of chopsticks.

"We play Magic the Gathering," said Roberto.

"What about the big boys?"

The spa therapist brought out a warm compress and placed it on his forehead.

"I haven't been back in a while. But from what I remember. Ah yes. In Catalonia, we have a game called find the marble. Don't laugh. But men in their prime working-age will gather along the meandering bricks of La Rambla. It's not because they want to or know any better, but because of tradition. I'm still young, but one day I too might don a nice leather jacket and cheer my teammates as they try to find the marble. Now there may be only three cups and one marble to find, but the shuffler goes very fast. He's had years to perfect his shell game. You have to keep your eyes on him the whole time and the team members cheer with so much gusto that it is easy to get lost in all the fun. And sometimes when tourists walk by, they are invited to play along."

"The simple things," Wishy-Wishy said. "I sure as hope…I can play that game too —if I ever go stomping my way to Spain." She stretched out the natto as high as her chopsticks could go.

"Barcelona," Roberto clarified. "La Rambla is in Barcelona and Barcelona is part of Catalonia. My parents lived in Catalonia. Including our two sisters, there are seven of us. We've moved seven times and somehow we ended up over here. My Mother, Antonia is from Caledonia and my Father is from Macedonia. They are always fighting. My Antonia makes most of the money so naturally, she wants a split and move to Patagonia."

"Could ya call yureself a Catalonian septenarius?"

"You mean separatist. Catalonian Separatist," Roberto corrected.

"Yure too young to vote anyhoo."

"You might say I'm how do they say here, wishy-washy? My older brother says we must separate. He wants his own apartment when he turns 18. He's five years older than me, and he is the most independent while my younger brother still relies on the love of our mother. He's still a mama's boy. Me, I'm in the middle."

"Aw shucks, ya shure sounds like Goldi-Locks."

"Yes, you might say I'm, Goldi-Locks." The way she spoke had rubbed him the wrong way, but he still tried to pay her a compliment. "You sound like you read a lot of books."

"Oh no. Don't read murch. Mostly simple booghs, nursery rhymes whatnot. I might could read more, but some wurds look like caterpillars to me. Hard enough to use the-mouz on the-wurd on the like, you know, dur-kapooter? Don't get me wrong. I'm mean, I've always wanted to mingle with macadamia."

He rubbed his temples. "I have a splitting headache." He wanted to cauterize his ears with a curling iron.

"I do declare I've got something that might could cure ya." Wishy-Wishy reached into her knapsack and took out a pyrex container. "I'll fix you up -guuud! ..with some Korean Black Ramen Chapagetti and seaweed."

Wishy-Wishy had a spa worker heat it up in a microwave and bring it out steaming hot. "Look at those strands. Yum, yum." It was a ramen-like noodle that was cooked then drained of most of its liquid before adding a chocolate-colored sauce that did not taste like chocolate. The way to eat it was to wrap it with bite-sized sheets of seaweed. She rolled up some noodles and gave it to Roberto. It was a completely new experience for him. Crispy on the outside, yet slightly chewy on the inside. His face brightened up as he took in the complex flavor profile that had hints of coffee, sesame oil, and something loving, satiating, that washed his headache away. Images of true friendship, a cozy home, and a stable family flashed through his mind.

"This taste. What is it?"

"It is umami, the fifth taste, discovered by Japanese food scientists, perfected in this Korean black noodle and seaweed combination." She let her accent slip and needed a quick recovery. "By golly, will ya look at the time."

The spa manager brought Mommy Dee the tab. It was time for Wishy-Wishy to retreat to an inner room to unmask.

"Listen, Roberto. I have a hootenanny to skedaddle to. Was a pleasure talking to ya."

"Pleasure was mine, Cleo." He closed his eyes and smiled under the drone of hypnotic music.

CHAPTER 13

THE POLLYWOGS

"Wishy-Wishy. Wake up from your slumber, honey. You have visitors," said Mommy Dee.

Wishy-Wishy didn't know it. She was popular. She was revered. So much so that three of her classmates took the town bus and showed up to her house one morning. Sean Karcher, Samantha Fontaine, and Zepherine Jones, her fellow classmates from Mr. Mathis' English class wanted to cheer her up. Wishy-Wishy hadn't been her usual self over the past week. She wasn't as attentive in class. She aimlessly walked the halls and kept to herself, sometimes speaking to a person that wasn't there.

"I don't understand. What are you guys doing here on a Sunday morning?" Wishy-Wishy asked.

Samantha looked up from below and said, "We each got an invitation. You mean it didn't come from you?"

"You're' more than welcome to play. In fact, I'd

love to play with you guys. But I didn't send anything of the sort," said Wishy-Wishy.

"But the message had your name on it," said Zepherine. It was a real head-scratcher.

"Someone must have spoofed your ID," said Sean.

The extent of their inquiry ended there. Once they saw the commode through the accordion doorway, the cargo net above, the fire pole, and a periscope that descended from a retractable conning tower, they knew they had to form a club either through squatting or by adverse possession. They nominated and elected Wishy-Wishy as president. Her house became the clubhouse. They called themselves the Pollywogs.

"We are but tadpoles," Samantha said. "Not that frogs have wings or anything, but one day we will grow up to become fully-fledged frogs."

"Or Cane toads." Said Zepherine."

They spent the better part of the morning playing freeze tag and tug o war. It became clear during freeze tag that Samantha Fontaine was the fastest sprinter. She could either tag everyone to make them "it" or outrun everyone and never became it. She was always the first one in any class to be done with her work or test or whatever it was she read. Sean Karcher, as it turned out, had a natural gift with anything that had to do with strings. He could find the connection between the most abstract things. He threaded a needle and showed Mommy Dee how to seamlessly French a seam. Zepherine had tireless stamina and true grit. His team in tug o war was always the winning team, even when it was a team on one. He pulled everyone else into the mud.

After a hosing off, a ho-down ensued. Sean took to the violin, then the guitar. He could play any string instrument thrown his way. They gathered by the fire pit and exchanged the usual unusual school gossip. They made bets on how long it would take Mr. Mathis to shrink to the size of a shrew. They questioned why there was only one GATE kid in the entire school. It seemed odd when Adrian Winklewort peered his eyes through the windows and said in a tiny, uneasy voice, "Hey guys…" The poor boy seemed lost, out of place. All everyone knew was that he was a GATE student, but there was no GATE cluster to speak of. He was a single GATE unit and a bit unhinged. Mr. Mathis scratched his head and invited him to fill the seat that had been empty the whole year in his English class. And what about Ezequio and his "condition?"

Mommy Dee brought out the marshmallows and graham crackers for the campfire s'mores.

After sinking her teeth into the gooey goodness, Samantha asked, "Is it true you can change people into something new just by saying a rhyme?"

"They have to say my name and I have to call them a rhyming nickname back. It's a two-way street and a double edge sword with no handle to grip so I don't recommend you ever say my full real name," Wishy-Wishy said. Samantha-banana came to mind, but Wishy-Wishy refrained herself for it would have caused a slip.

Then Samantha asked Wishy-Wishy about Ezequio. Wishy-Wishy felt like she had been asked the same question before. She already had what seemed like an uncannily canned answer. Instead of answering it, she turned the tables and said to Samantha, "I don't want to talk about Ezequio right now. The boy has issues. But what I do want to know is why did you guys choose me as pollywog president? I have no strength or any practical skills in life."

"How wrong you are," said Sean. "There is a Bavarian phrase called spandes bagan. It literally translates to 'bow span'. If you want to go far in life, you will need to pull your bowstring as far back as you can pull, and then further. It may not seem like you are making any progress, and you won't see any results for a long time. Those who let go of their string too soon will, at best, break even. Those who pull too far back and never let go will lose everything in one snap.

Only the rightful owner can restring his or her bow. Now you might think that you are not up to snuff compared to the rest of us." He flexed his biceps. "But can anyone take a guess as to which sport in the ancient Olympiads garnered the highest honor?"

Wishy-Wishy saw in Samantha, Sean, and Zepherine -perfect specimens of jocks with brains.

"Would it be the hundred-meter dash?" Samantha asked.

"Quick to win and quickly forgotten. The metric system wasn't around back then," said Sean.

"What about Greco Roman wrestling?" Zepherine asked.

"Wrestling takes a lot of strength, but it is not wrestling that's worth the pence. The period of time I'm talking about predates the Roman influence," Sean added.

"The javelin," said Wishy-Wishy.

"A javelin may lance the heart of a lion, but it won't melt the heart of the Sun."

"I give up," Wishy-Wishy said.

"The Olympics represented the perfection of the mind and body. There were athletes of amazing gifts, but the highest honor was bestowed on the poet," said Sean. "Poetry was a team sport. It required rigorous training and a full-time coach. From the din of odes and soliloquies arose the poet warrior." He had sewn for Wishy-Wishy a laurel crown. He bit off a stray thread with his teeth and placed it on her head.

"I am flattered, Sean Karcher, but I don't think I am deserving of such a title, nor is it something I wish to rest upon," Wishy-Wishy said.

"But do wear your crown. I have fashioned it like a barrette or a fancy hairpiece, depending on how you wish to wear it. It will look fabulous on you. The first half is a laurel crown while the back half is like a stretchy string you can use to shape your locks."

"I will wear it until I run into someone worthy. I will be keeper of the crown."

"Fair enough," said Sean.

Wishy-Wishy tried it on. It brought her hair mostly into a ponytail. In normal mode, it served as a barrette, just as Sean said. It went well with her upside down knitted sweater, Osh-Kosh overalls, and writing instruments both sharp and dull. But when Samantha took the time to properly arrange Wishy-Wishy's raven tress, it left columns of hair on either side, like the flying buttresses of a cosmic cathedral. It complemented well her grandmother's yellow dress. "You're right Sean. It looks splendid. Thank you," Wishy-Wishy said.

"You look fit for a coronation. But don't worry.

No one will know what it means except for us Pollywogs," said Samantha.

As the evening died down, Samantha pulled Wishy-Wishy aside for a walk and asked her a personal question. It was not about Ezequio, but about someone else, an imagined being.

"Wishy-Wishy. Do you have someone to confide with? Besides Daddy Joe and Mommy Dee, I mean. It's just that at school. I've seen you sitting at your favorite table. Mouth moving. Pushing air."

"Was it that obvious?"

"Nothing wrong with that. I talk to myself often when I have a brain teaser to solve."

"Perhaps I was unknowingly talking to my imaginary sister like I did when I was younger. She doesn't have a name. I just called her sister."

"Listen. I am always here if you can't keep a secret or want to spill the beans on something, especially when it comes to boys and how to avoid them."

It caught Wishy-Wishy by surprise. "Oh. Thank you kindly," she said respectfully. "I will do the same for you then." She did not tell her how lonely she sometimes got. So lonely that she had to make up an imaginary sister.

She did not confide much with Samantha. Sometimes it was like that. Meet the right person, and her inner secrets would flow like Niagra Falls. Not that Samantha was intrusive or anything. Perhaps Samantha was too diplomatic in her approach, and for that very reason, Wishy-Wishy tended to be cordial with her.

Aside from the awkward conversation, Wishy-Wishy had a splendid Sunday. At least she won't have to pretend to be talking to someone again. How did she find such wonderful friends? Wishy-Wishy wondered. Or rather, how did they find her? She had dismissed them as a cliquish group of enlightened jocks. She recalled an entire hour watching Zepherine peel and eat his own fore-arm scab as Mr. Mathis shuffled his jowls while reciting the *Rime of the Ancient Mariner*. The boy could never find a pair of matching socks. She went to bed grateful after Commodore Joe drove the house to drop them off one by one. She slept at home on the way back home and not that many people could do that.

CHAPTER 14

THE BOY WHO MADE HER CRY

The next day Wishy-Wishy wore her grand mother's yellow dress and her new hairpiece that Sean had made for her. She was the most beautiful girl in school. She wasn't worried about the gawkers. Why should school attire be limited to jeans and overalls? She wanted to do her Pollywogs proud.

Her squonk would have none of it. He never made eye contact, but that morning was different. There was a thick overcast, but no rain. He stood there against the wall, looked at her eyes, and rasped the chain link fence three times with his nails. Wishy-Wishy didn't know what to make of it. When she didn't do anything, he rasped it again three times.

"Okay. So you want me to rasp this thing three times." She rasped the fence three times. It didn't sound as creepy as his rendition for he had nails that could harm a raccoon. "Do you have an itch to scratch or something?" She couldn't recall ever losing a fight with a squonk.

Then he scratched the downspout of a gutter three times, followed by three flicks to the window.

"Oh. So you want to play a game." Wishy-Wishy scratched the gutter three times, followed by three flicks to the window. He ran across the hallway and waited. Strangely enough, she followed him. He cupped his hands as if hiding something. Every time she wanted to see, he turned his back to her and marveled at its beauty all to himself.

"Sharing is caring. Let me see, let me see," she said. "You're just teasing me. There's nothing there."

He turned to her and opened his hands. Out flew a dozen yellow and blue tiger swallowtails. These butterflies flapped their showy wings, circled about and landed again in his palms. They liked to wick the moisture from his muddy hands. He blew them on her face and they tickled her nose. He ran to a door and knocked three times. She knocked three times. The more sounds they made, the more butterflies appeared. They slapped on a mat with a rat-tat-tat. They turned duck-duck-goose into ding-dong-ditch. They played tic-tac-toe-toe with an ugly stick. He took her hands and spun her around until she became dizzy. She did the same to him, and they both became tipsy. They tapped on the bins with a rin-tin-tin. They hopped toe to toe like an Eskimo. They did the side-side skip to

the lou, then WHOOSH. He swept her off her feet
and onto his back and spread his arms like the wings
of an eagle. They chased a blizzard of butterflies
between drafty corridors and classes in progress, past
hall guards with rattling whistles, through Earth
Science and Home Ec, through Pre Algebra and Band,
leaving gusts of sheet music and tardy slips. They
fluttered in one classroom, out another and across the
cloven quad.

Then, when she was laughing with giddiness, he set
her down. It was at a picnic table with a bird's eye
view of the quad. He took her hand and had her take
a seat.

"I didn't realize I could have so much fun with a
squonk."

He was not yet done. He had but one final act. He
tapped the table three times. She tapped three times.

"Are you trying to tell me something?"

He held her hands. He looked into her eyes and
she did the same. He had wet eyes of a Shitzu. And
then he did the last thing a squonk was expected to do.
He summoned what strength he had to awaken
muscles that never worked before, the ones he was
born with but never used. He smiled through his
yellow teeth.

She was delighted a squonk could smile, so she

smiled back.

He pursed his lips.

She pursed her lips.

He closed his eyes.

She closed her eyes.

And before she could make any sense of it, he vanished. All that was left was a fine coat of morning dew.

Wishy-Wishy walked back to class smiling, blushing. She was once again a fine mess, more so than usual, and she could care less. Her hair had come undone. She spun her laurel like a tassel and relived the sequence in her mind, the fence rasping, the gutter scratching, the window flicking, the knock-knock-knock, the rat-tat-tat and the ding-dong-ditch, the tic-tac-toe and the ugly stick, the dipsy-tipsy spinning and the rin-tin-tin, the hopping toe to toe and the Eskimo, the side-side skip and the eagle high flying, and the tabletop tapping. But the smiling and the pursing of the lips she kept repeating until her traipse turned into a stagger, then a standstill. Then emptiness. She didn't make it back to class. She ran straight home, crying all the way and she didn't know why.

"What did he say to you?" asked Mommy Dee.

"He didn't say a thing."

"Your clothes are muddy again. Did he hurt you?"

"No. I'm crying, but. I mean no."

"What did you guys do?"

"We played. We danced. We flew to the moon. And then. When he set me down, we smiled. I was so happy and then the feeling went away, and all I felt was emptiness, and sadness, like something was missing, but it had everything and nothing to do with him."

"You're not making any sense," said Daddy Joe.

"Did he...dump you?" Mommy Dee asked.

"No. I mean. I don't know. It's not like I like him. He's so gross."

"Did he try to kiss you?" Mommy Dee asked anxiously.

"Yes. I mean No. It wasn't like that at all." She took a breath.

Mommy Dee and Daddy Joe looked at each other and said, "Hormones."

"Ewww!" Wishy-Wishy shrieked and went up to her room. Not even Bob-Betsy and Bob-Bella could help her figure this one out. When presented with either flakes or pellets, they darted up to take their fill and then retreated to the comfort of their cave. None of the books she ever read could prepare her for this. She could parse the meaning of words with a fine-tooth comb, but in the end, she came undone by a wordless squonk. "Is this what it means to have a relationship with a squonk?" She wondered. She supposed she was the only one in the world to have ever danced with a squonk, much less seen one smile. It was all too much for her to handle. If she was to survive the school year, Wishy-Wishy figured she had best avoid him. But then she saw in her mind again the smiling and the pursing of the lips, not his, but someone else's. She had seen it before. But where? And when?

She turned to her left while laying in bed and noticed the straight line of her eye-level bookshelf was not straight, but interrupted by a thin gleaming rectangle, half an inch in length. As she sat up, an oval took its place, then a circle. It was a golden ring. She picked up the ring and read the letters engraved on the surface. "A.N. 8391"

"Wonder how it got here," she said.

CHAPTER 15

SUSPENSION OF DISBELIEF

It was not until Wishy-Wishy went back to school the next day and sat at her usual picnic table that it all made sense. She repeated the tapping on the table. She did not notice it the other day, but she had already touched the very thing her squonk wanted her to see. Written in shorthand, a language few could read, was the note:

Adhyaksa & Wishy-Wishy -Sisters forever.

"Adhyaksa," Wishy-Wishy mouthed. She ran through the quad. "ADHYAKSA! ADHYAKSA! ADHYAKSA!"

Francisco Roberto Romero was walking to class when his brother Francisco said to his ear, "O hark O hear. Is that Cleopatra in the rear?" They turned around and saw the girl they met at the spa. "She doesn't have that southern split in her tongue, but I do smell the same pencil, the Great Lakes cedar and Sri Lankan graphite," said Francisco.

"How is it that Cleopatra still remembers Adhyaksa?" Francisco asked. "Is Cleopatra special? Would she make good source material?"

"The Jabberwock does not like it when we present him with false positives," said Roberto.

"The Gate cluster was not exactly to his liking," said Francisco. "They've been facsimilized into serpents and disguised as their former selves, ready to bite at our command. All we need to do is rattle our whistle."

"I have an idea. We will start a tutoring club," said Roberto.

"Brilliant," said Romero.

"Now what to do about Cleopatra?" Francisco asked.

"She is a guarded young lady. We must first gain her trust. Test her," said Roberto. "First we invite her."

"And if she has the light of a thousand eyes?" Francisco asked.

"Then we bite her," said Romero.

"Right," said Roberto.

They went about their business of creating a lunch 'n learn tutoring club, which wasn't too difficult. Roberto had recently transferred from another school and was already Mrs. Figgleworth's favorite student. He had the rare ability to solve complex math problems with his right hand and write rhetorical English essays with his left hand, all while carrying on a conversation with whoever he happened to be speaking with. He had both the art and faculty of discovering the best possible means of persuasions with regard to any subject, whatever. He had brought an apple to class earlier that day. It wasn't long before Mrs. Figgleworth gave him permission to use her room to operate his tutoring club. He would not be the only one to do the tutoring, Roberto explained. The first order of business was to recruit the brightest students he could find.

"What a lovely idea," Mrs. Figgleworth said. "I will mention this in our next PTA meeting. I will ask every board member to volunteer their brightest students to become a tutor."

❋ ❋ ❋

"...ADHYAKSA!...ADHYAKSA!... ADHYAKSA! I remember you. I remember," shouted Wishy-Wishy.

Samantha heard Wishy-Wishy from across the breezeway.

"What's wrong, Wishy-Wishy?"

"Have you seen Adhyaksa?"

"Adhy-who?"

"Adhyaksa."

"That's a pretty name, but I don't know who you're talking about."

"How can you not know? Adhyaksa sits in our English class where Adrian now sits."

"I'm sorry Wishy-Wishy, but that chair was always empty until Adrian showed up."

"I'm not imagining this. Adhyaksa is my best friend."

At that moment, Samantha knew she had to tread carefully. "I see. I will keep an eye out for her then," said Samantha in a measured tone.

The way Samantha said it made Wishy-Wishy feel uncomfortable.

"Oh never mind," Wishy-Wishy said. "I'm just a lunatic with an imaginary friend."

Wishy-Wishy took off running the other way and didn't stop until she reached her English class, which was not yet in session. Peeking through the window, she thought back to the last time she saw Adhyaksa. It was shortly after she had wrestled the report card from her squonk. She was calling Ezequio a wet blanket, then what happened within that space of time she couldn't recall. It was as if someone took a scalpel, sliced out a piece of time and tucked it away from the watchful eyes of the universe. She knocked herself on the head a few times. Why haven't I noticed my missing best friend these couple of days?

Adhyaksa wasn't the first person to go missing for a week. Something similar happened to Ezequio, she thought. But she never gave Adhyaksa a nickname. This gave Wishy-Wishy pause. She remembered Mr. Mathis mentioning how students have been known to go missing for days on end only to show up again as if the days on end never existed. Mr. Mathis should know more about this, she thought.

When Wishy-Wishy arrived at Mr. Mathis' office, he was nowhere to be seen. Then a voice said from down below, "Over here." He had shrunken to the size of a guinea pig and wore the remains of his lunch on his shirt while bits of cornbread clung to his mustache like sawdust. He wasn't in a jovial mood.

"How could you let it come to this?"

"I'm sorry Wishy-Wishy. I was out last night and they had an open mic. So I took to the stage and cracked some corny jokes. I couldn't help myself."

"Did they get a good laugh?"

"Yeah, I suppose so."

"That's all that matters. But seriously, you're going

to disappear one day, and it won't be funny at all."

He climbed a rope ladder to his swivel chair. Once there, he was still too short to see above his desk. "It's no use," he lamented.

"Why don't I pick you up. It would be easier to talk to you." She reached out her hands and allowed him to climb on.

"What brings you here so early in the day? You usually take some time to settle in and don't get into trouble until 10 am."

"Do you know what happened to Adhyaksa?"

"Who's that?" Mr. Mathis asked with a straight face.

"Adhyaksa, the Indian girl who sits next to me in class."

"I'm sorry. I don't know who you are talking about."

"I get that a lot."

Mr. Mathis scratched his head. His hair seemed shinier than normal. "Wait a minute. Does anyone else besides you know of this Adhyaksa girl, that she is missing?"

"I brought up her name to Samantha, and she didn't know what I was talking about. She thought Adhyaksa was an imaginary friend, someone I made up because that's what pathetic loners do."

"Listen. If you've told people you lost a friend, the fact that you have the courage to do so could only mean that Adhyaksa indeed existed and that she is not a figment of your imagination. You needn't mention it to anyone else. It would just make you sound looney."

"Why do you believe me all of a sudden?"

Mr. Mathis slumped on Wishy-Wishy's hands. "Because I too have lost some friends when I was in school, and no one believed me."

"What happened to your friends?" Wishy-Wishy asked.

"The Jabberwock happened."

"You're talking about that creature from Lewis Carroll's Through the Looking Glass, aren't you?" She had seen an etched line drawing of a dragon-like beast with long whiskers and antennas and a little girl holding the handle of a long and heavy sword. She could never tell whether Alice would swing the sword to strike the Jabberwock or if the sword was too heavy and would pull the little girl back.

"Then you know about the jubjub bird."

"And the tumtum tree."

"I don't know about that Jabberwock, but this one is very real. He thrives on imagination, so he seeks out the creative types, the over-achievers. He has no friends, so he seeks out those who are popular, bends them to his will. He's too lazy to do his own bookkeeping, so he seeks out math wizards and forces them to do mundane ledger entries. The only way one could defeat a Jabberwock is with pure wit. Only with pure wit can you conjure up a vorpal blade. Only with a vorpal blade can you slay him. Before you can take him down, you'll have to defeat his minions. Each generation must face their own demons. I have slain the Jabberwock in my time. It is up to you to do the same."

"Will you help me find Adhyaksa?"

"I will do what I can with what little time I have. We will need to gather as many remaining clues about Adhyaksa in this world before it disappears forever. The more we know about her, the better our chances of building a strong connection to her whereabouts and her whenabouts. Do you know where she lived?"

"454 Obsidian View," said Wishy-Wishy. "And she forgot her ring when she visited my house." Wishy-Wishy showed Mr. Mathis the golden ring.

"It's a good thing you knew her well enough to know her address, and you have something that belongs to her. That's a good start."

"We dropped her off after a play date, but I've never actually been inside her house. Been meaning to visit, but haven't got around to it. She did describe her place to me."

Mr. Mathis called Ms. Gertrude and asked her if she would be his substitute for English class. Wishy-Wishy placed Mr. Mathis inside her chest pocket and made for the door. "You don't drive your car anymore, I take it."

"I've been taking the bus for some time now. My car battery died from me not being able to reach the ignition. I find public transit much easier on the pocketbook, though I really should pay off my economy car. I must say, it has been more challenging lately, relying on the kindness of strangers for a pick-me-up."

"I thought you and Ms. Gertrude were…" She paused for she knew she was trudging into his personal life.

"Oh yes. Ms. Gertrude Greensleeves. She is nice enough to pick me up as in literally picking me up like a little child and swinging me gleefully through the air, but that is the extent of our relationship. It's an arrangement, you see. Strictly professional. She misses the days of swinging a small child, and I miss the days of climbing on trees…as a small child and I should leave it at that."

"One could do worse than be a swinger of birches."

The Green-line bus rolled up like a hungry horntail

caterpillar. It expelled a few and swallowed a few. Wishy-Wishy found a place near the back of the bus and had a seat.

"Why is it that no one on this bus or in school is startled about your size?" Wishy-Wishy asked.

"It's called suspension of disbelief. It's hard to explain," said Mr. Mathis.

"Sorry about my prying back there. I didn't mean to intrude," Wishy-Wishy said, knowing darn well the speech act she had committed to make Mr. Mathis unload some more juicy bits.

"Not a problem." Mr. Mathis took a deep breath then continued, "After I killed the Jabberwock and brought everyone back into the world, I discovered that not everyone's memories had survived. Some had instantly reunited with friends and loved ones while others took time to adjust, but they eventually remembered each other and made themselves whole again."

"And Ms. Gertrude?"

"When you look at someone you've known, you look for acknowledgment in their eyes. But when I looked into her hazel eyes, she did not recognize who I was. She greeted me with the same polite hellos and nothing more. And to think she was the reason I went on my quest to slay the Jabberwock. But I can't blame her for not remembering me. It wasn't her fault. What was I supposed to say? It is I, Roy Mathis who had rescued you from the Jabberwock and now I must tell you everything. I will tell you all -but show not tell they always used to say. How could I show what was forgotten?" Mr. Mathis looked out the window as the peanut fields turned back into residential blocks. "I left plenty of bread crumbs, but she never picked them up." He let out a breath that fogged up the window for a moment. "She found happiness with someone else. I never mustered the courage to ask her out again, but that's okay. Her happiness was what mattered most to me. Graduation came and we went our separate ways. Sometimes you lose something in victory."

"That is the saddest story I've ever heard. And who but Lady Greensleeves would show up at our school again as a substitute teacher. Was it just to torment you?"

"I should have been a pair of ragged claws scuttling across the floor of silent seas."

"Is she married?"

"Same last name, but you know how it is these days. I'm afraid to ask —afraid to find out. How would I begin? —When I am a pygmy half-pint pet of a teacher's pet. (ᴄ‿ᴐ) And how should I presume? —When she is an Amazon, as tall as the moon. Every time I see her in a room, I'm just a fumbling bumbling buffoon with nothing but nonsense to say."

"Tell me, Mr. Mathis. Hast thou slain the Jabberwock?"

"No. It appears I have not. I only thought I did." He let out a sigh.

"But she does pick you up and that makes you sooo happy."

"Yes, she does," agreed Mr. Mathis.

"And that's what we call suspension of disbelief," Wishy-Wishy said while poking him in the tummy (DOINK).

He giggled like the Pillsbury doughboy. "I suppose you're right. Listen. I may have lost someone special, but I will not let the same thing happen to you and your friends."

"You can never lose someone who's always in your heart," said Wishy-Wishy.

The bus pulled to a stop at a strip mall. Wishy-Wishy walked a few blocks with Mr. Mathis in her chest pocket until she found herself in a residential neighborhood. She strolled along the even-numbered side of Obsidian View until the digits grew from the one hundreds to the three hundreds. Just as Adhyaksa had described, the neighborhood was home to shot-gun bungalows of various shapes and sizes. As she approached the four hundreds, she saw something shimmering in the sky. Wishy-Wishy realized that her friend lived in anything but a bungalow. Why didn't she see this when she dropped her off? It was an imposing structure, 15 stories high, towering sheets of mirrored glass, marble cladding, and translucent concrete. Each planted floor swiveled on its own axis like the blades of a pixie wheel facing the sky. She wondered how such a thing could get by the zoning commission.

There was no visible door, only a numerical keypad at eye level below and a brushed aluminum awning above their heads.

"It looks like we need a code to enter," said Wishy-Wishy. She took a closer look and noticed a doorbell. How would she crack the code?

Wishy-Wishy rang the doorbell, and when no one answered, she took the golden ring and punched the numbers 8391 into the keypad with the eraser end of her number 2 pencil. It didn't work.

"You're the only one in class with a sharp pencil left," said Mr. Mathis. "What are you saving it for?"

"I've yet to make my point." She punched in 4548391#.

They heard a humming sound from inside followed by the adhesive separation of an air-tight seal as the door rolled up into the ceiling.

"Isn't this breaking and entering?" Wishy-Wishy said. The positive air pressure rushed out of the building.

"We didn't break anything. And I would hardly call this a home, but rather a simulacrum of an idealized living arrangement," Mr. Mathis explained as Wishy-Wishy walked beyond the threshold and into the lobby. "It is the type of property where people will pine over on social media, but nobody in their right mind would live here."

The color palette was cool and inviting. The shades of teal and sea-foam said stay awhile and have a chat. No rush. At the same time, the postmodern furniture and cushions looked immaculate, like no one had ever sat on them for fear of messing up a picture-perfect scene. Wishy-Wishy looked up and saw fourteen floors rotating like flower petals on a pixie wheel and got dizzy. It reminded her of Ezequio's Tuscan villa, but worse.

At the center stood a crystal spiral escalator. They could see through the walls and into the suites as they passed through one floor after another. Each flat had its own artistic biome: Botticelli, Monét, Dali, O'keefe, Picasso, Van Gogh, Kandinsky, Warhol, Wright, Banksy, Gaudi, and Liechtenstein. Soon enough they saw chrome rabbits that must have cost a pretty penny. When they reached the top floor, the layout was still that of a bungalow, but a pink ray of light from a Kinkade painting was closing in. It wouldn't be long before a pretentious sophistication would replace the warm feeling of home.

"We have to act fast before it's too late," Mr. Mathis said.

As Wishy-Wishy ran through the kitchen, generic appliances became stainless steel, built-in, and so fancy that the brand names fell off and only a connoisseur would know what they were looking at. The lights retreated into new recesses, and the shag carpeting turned into velour. An Archie Bunker burlap sofa morphed into a sleek chaise. The socks on the floor organized themselves into Marie Condo stacks on cedar shelves.

Wishy-Wishy made her way to Adhyaksa's bed, pulled open the drawers, and snatched a journal from the nightstand before the bogus religiosity could creep in. She held it close to her heart and made for the spiral escalator. Only one problem, the escalator only seemed to go up.

"There must be a way to go down," she said.

A computer voice asked, "Do you wish to go down?"

"Yes. As fast as we can," said Wishy-Wishy.

"Very well," said the voice.

The transparent steps of the spiral escalator adjusted themselves until rise over run became zero. Wishy-Wishy slid screaming down the dizzying pillar to the first floor where an automatic floor simonizing machine had left a slick sheen of mild soap on the tiles, before turning around for the drying round. The floor became a slip'n slide which Wishy-Wishy rode all the way out the front door.

"We hope you enjoyed your stay," said the polite computer voice as the door sealed itself shut.

CHAPTER 16

SHEEP-A-VOID

Later that night, Wishy-Wishy played her favorite board game with Daddy Joe and Mommy Dee. She wanted to brush up on her game-playing skills.

Farmer McTavish kept a drove of killer sheep that will ruin a slumber party by knocking you to sleep as they hop the picket fence, roll down the hill and smother you with their wooly warmth. The best way to avoid a sheep in SHEEP-A-VOID is to void a sheep by creating a void in the hill for the sheep to fall into and then move out of the way. Most sheep roll straight downhill, but a black sheep can roll in any direction, even against gravity. Whoever stayed up the latest and counted the most sheep won the game. SHEEP-A-VOID was immensely popular in Australia, but not so much in Ireland.

She said to Daddy Joe while rolling the dodecahedron dice and picking up a milk card, "I do miss playing this game. Almost as fun as when we sang Commodore Joe."

"Oh, that silly song. I can't believe you still remember. You were just The Chubican in need of potty training."

So it was true. Daddy Joe had forgotten the reprise just a few weeks ago, how they sang Commodore Joe to Adhyaksa and how Daddy Joe tooted his personal fog horn. This ship had sailed and left Adjyaksa at port.

Daddy Joe counted the most sheep in SHEEP-A-VOID, which meant Wishy-Wishy had to go to bed. Before counting her own sheep, she gave Daddy Joe and Mommy Dee an unusually long hug.

Looking up through the porthole window, Wishy-Wishy caught a glimpse of Venus just below the crescent moon. She wondered if Adhyaksa's parents back in Hyderabad knew they had another daughter. Did her sisters notice the extra room in bed five years ago? Would the house seem a tad bit quieter all along? Would they have wished for another child?

"Now what?" The only item Wishy-Wishy was able to retrieve from Adhyaksa's room was the journal. Wishy-Wishy didn't know if she should read it. On the one hand, it was Adhyaksa's personal log and to read it without her permission would be to intrude on her inner sanctum. But it was Adhyaksa who was the nosiest one of them all, why with her IP spoofing and hacking and interloping and intrusive questions about Ezequio and her unreal knowledge of the strengths of each member of the Pollywogs. The only way to find Adhyaksa was to know more about her. As Wishy-Wishy soon found out, Adhyaksa's journal had very little to do with the writer.

The first page read:

Dear Sister Wishy-Wishy,

If you find this book it would mean I am no longer attending school with you. I will have been back home in Hyderabad, tending to our flock of sheep. Just kidding. More like fighting with my birth sisters on who gets the top bunk all to herself. I spend more time than I should, watching people and noting different things about them. I've taken the time to catalogue the student body to help guide you in making new friends in my absence. I've already sent three of them your way. Use this as a rough guide, but not as a substitute for getting to know them.

Love,

Adhyaksa

P.S. Stay safe from the beasties and keep this bestiary of besties close to thy breasty. (My first rhyme. Don't you love it?)

Adhyaksa assigned every kid she came across a code and plotted their qualities along a 3 axis chart. Every student had a certain number of hit points. It was no surprise that Zepherine would have 3,000 hit points while someone like Samantha would have a lot of speed and agility. Wishy-Wishy found it disturbing that Adhyaksa gave her 1 hit point and 3 measly units of strength, which would make her completely useless in a role-playing battle. Equally perplexing was how next to each unit of measure for Ezequio were the letters "unk" for unknown. All she listed were his weaknesses which were his general malaise, tendency to cry, and aversion to the sun.

Wishy-Wishy rubbed her temple and closed the book. She didn't know how this book was supposed to help her find Adhyaksa. It looked like it was trying to set up a new kind of role-playing game where the stakes were high. But just when she was about to get to the juicy bits, the words changed to some characters she could not recognize.

Wishy-Wishy never had any patience for grinding away at role-playing games, much less a live-action one. Nor did she have the ability to keep track of stats.

If a group of geeks invited her on a larping campaign, she would just as well cast life on everyone, as in "get a life," and the game would abruptly come to an end as everyone would pick up the pieces and move on with their lives. Before long, the sheep she counted knocked her into bed, and she fell fast asleep.

Morning came and school became an uncomfortable place again.

"There she goes talking to her imaginary friend," someone said in the distance. She tried to pay no attention to it.

In English class, Wishy-Wishy looked across the classroom and saw not a sqounk, but the boy who made her cry the other day. She finally knew what Ezequio was trying to tell her with his interpretive dance number, that she had a friend. Her name was Adhyaksa. She brought her such happiness. And if she cried as much as she did before realizing the loss of her friend, she couldn't imagine what he had been feeling since the beginning of the school year. She remembered the look in his eyes when he fell to the ground after smearing mud on her face. She realized Ezequio had lost his mother to the Jabberwock, but could never share his feelings with a world that wouldn't believe. She hated herself for turning Ezequio into a squonk and couldn't bear to have his puppy eyes looking back at her. She had to get some fresh air.

"Where are you going?" Zepherine asked.

"Leave her be," said Samantha. "She has some things to suss out. You can lose a friend in real life, but an imaginary friend? Those are the toughest to get over," she said under her breath.

Wishy-Wishy heard some of Samantha's comment as she stepped out the door. It seemed no one class would believe her either if she were to tell them about her missing friend.

Wishy-Wishy walked back in, picked up Mr. Mathis, set him aside, grabbed hold of the podium and moved it out of the way. It was just her alone, facing her classmates, gazing into their eyes. She tried to convince them the only way she knew how. She closed her eyes and made a wish. Then she improvised a song on the spot.

Not..just
In my head
In my mind
I would hope
You could play with me.

I..would
Visit your
Neighborhood
If I could
Hands..in..my pocket
Find the golden ring!

Ad-hy-ak-sa
I'll do anything
You back home
I will bring
Four-five-four
Four-five-four-five-four…

At your door now
Hear the door bell ring
Four-five-four
Ding-dong-ding
Four-five-four
Four-five-four-five-four…

Four-five-four
I can sing
Four-five-four
Four-five-four-five-four…

❀ ❀ ❀

What did it mean? Nobody knew. But the tone of the song, the vulnerability, the determination, the way she sang it moved Zepherine from sadness to hope.

"She did lose someone," Samantha said. Before Samantha could say anything more, Wishy-Wishy walked out the door and didn't return to class.

Mr. Mathis had given Wishy-Wishy an infinite hall pass the day before when they stepped out of the bus. "Use this to clear your mind whenever you feel the weight of the world on your shoulders." With this slip of paper, she could wander around school anytime she wanted. There would be no repercussions for being late or walking in or out of any class whenever she felt like it. She was free to leave her flock.

She had placed Adhyaksa's bestiary in her locker for safekeeping when her squonk caught up with her. His speech, while sparse in the beginning, was now reduced to a few grunts and squeals. "Ezequio. Can you go back to class?"

"GRUNT-GRUNT. I believe. GRUNT-GRUNT. I believe."

"That's just swell," Wishy-Wishy said with little enthusiasm.

"SQUEAL."

"Mr. Mathis has an important lesson to teach today about Xerxes and his horrible loss at the Gates of

Thermopylae." Wishy-Wishy placed her hand on his shoulder. "I know you want to play but I cannot dance with you today. There's too much sunlight. She picked up a lump of mud and smeared it on his chin. Maybe when the skies are doomy and gloomy…you could be my sunshine once more." She could only manage half a sheepish smile. "Why, who knows who else I will remember if I were to feel alive again?"

He simpered then he whimpered and shuffled the other way.

Wishy-Wishy walked aimlessly, trying to clear her mind. She soon found herself in the athletic realm. The seventh-grade girls played tennis and practiced their backhand while learning the art of avoiding love. She wandered onto the football field. Before long, a wave of boys passed on by. Then, trotting along at a leisurely pace was Francisco Roberto Romero. He was too cool to break a sweat. When he reached her, he jogged in place.

"Would you care to join me for a pleasure run? It's something to treasure. A run. At your own leisure, for pleasure."

Why not? She thought. Maybe a pleasure run could be her *Balm of Gilead*. It might just do her some good.

It was awfully bright out there on the tracks.

Roberto skipped sideways on the long ends of the track, always facing normal to the sun. "This is how we run the 440 in Granada, muchacha. When prancing south, we face the window sills on the hobo hills. When lancing north, we say ooh-la-la to the grandmamas at The Alhambra." He blew a kiss into the air.

"I never knew that," said Wishy-Wishy, copying his side to side gallop.

What was more impressive was how Roberto did not have to open his mouth at all while running.

"I've trained so well, I don't have to breathe." He closed his mouth and pinched his nose shut for the length of the track.

"No wonder you call it a pleasure run," panted Wishy-Wishy.

"You are the same, but not the same girl we met the other day."

"You mean not so colorful?"

"Nothing wrong with a Southern drawl; it's what you say with a Southern drawl, Cleopatra."

"Oh. You still remember my alias."

"You mean Cleo is not short for Cleopatra?"

"My name is Wishy-Wishy. Before that, it was Jane. And before that, I will not say."

"Wishy-Wishy then it is. Nice to finally meet you

again. By the way. How are you with your studies?"

It seemed off-topic why he would ask her about her grades, but she answered, "I get A's in everything, except English. Never managed anything but a C this year."

"In case you're interested, I've started a tutoring club."

"Amazing," said Wishy-Wishy.

"You're going to want better grades if you are to enter a good institution. We call it Tag-Team-Tutoring. Each pre-teen seeking tutelage has the attention of two talented tutors tutoring them for twenty-two minutes and twenty-two seconds during lunch. You can either be a mentor or a mentee. What will it be?"

"I'm not sure," she said. "What's it like?"

"Tell you what. You can help yourself as a helper or help someone else be a helper."

Just as he handed her a tiny flyer, the winds shifted, and Wishy-Wishy caught a whiff of *au naturel*, that strange smell she could not place. It made her nauseated and arrested her breathing. She stopped in her tracks and took a spritz from her asthma inhaler.

"Listen, Roberto. It has been a pleasure running with you. But I need to get back to class before I make the news. I'll be sure to drop by your tutoring club someday." She walked upwind and away as quick as she could.

Roberto resumed his relaxing stride and began to breathe again. He said to his invisible brothers, "Your breaths smell like a Roman sewer. I told you not to open your mouths around people. And I told you not to eat La Rambla sewer rats or just rats in general in La Rambla. They don't digest too well, and you can't regurgitate them either."

"Some of us need to do the breathing and the sweating, seeing how Mr. Suave never seems to do it," Francisco said.

"A serpent Naga King has seven heads and I a prince but three. 'Bring me the light of a thousand eyes,' the Jabberwock said, and he will restore me to my former glory," Roberto said while catching up with his class.

Wishy-Wishy couldn't get over the extrastenchilism emanating from Roberto. She didn't want to know which part(s) it came from. But then she realized if any kid knew about role-playing games, it had to be Francisco Roberto Romero. More importantly, what kind of game would the strengths and weakness found in Adhyaksa's book lend themselves to best?

CHAPTER 17

THE LIGHT OF A THOUSAND EYES

Wishy-Wishy didn't know why her squonk acted up at lunch break. She took her sack lunch and was making her way to Mrs. Figgleworth's classroom when her squonk grabbed her by the ankle and wouldn't let go.

"Well, this is hardly productive," she said while placing her hand on her hips. "How am I supposed to find Adhyaksa if I don't dig deeper?"

"Don't..go. Don't..go."

She grabbed hold of a pillar and wrestled herself into the sun until her squonk could bear it no more and released his grip.

The last words she heard from him while walking across the sunny quad was, "Beware the shadows..." It seemed odd coming from a squonk who hated the sun.

Wishy-Wishy brought Adhyaksa's book into Roberto's tutoring session.

"Welcome to Tag Team Tutoring," said Roberto.

"How can you help or be helped today?

"I would like to watch for a while," said Wishy-Wishy.

"As you wish."

The desks in the room ran along two rows. Among them sat two rows of tutors in folding chairs. GATE students volunteered their time for one group while another group consisted students who came recommended by Lewis PTA board members. Wishy-Wishy would have been among the volunteers for Lady Gertrude suggested that she too become a tutor. But Wishy-Wishy was too modest, so she demurred on the recommendation. There was another group of GATE kids who acted like they needed tutoring and actively sought out help from the non-GATE tutors.

"Do you like what you see?" Roberto asked

"Students helping students achieve. I'm impressed," said Wishy-Wishy. "I'm trying to figure something out, and I wonder if you can help me."

"Is it related to school?"

"Yes and no. You did mention how you liked to play live-action role-playing games in Barcelona."

His eyes lit up. "Of course. Grab a table, and I'll be with you shortly," said Roberto.

There was but one remaining desk at the far end of the classroom facing the doorway. Wishy-Wishy walked past the kids and heard the students ask all manner of questions to their overwhelmed tutors. The questions ranged from the speed of light in molasses to 'would you rather…?'

On yet another table, Wishy-Wishy heard a GATE student ask his tutor if she could help him solve the infamous Chinese family crossing a river puzzle, the one where there was only one boat and a cop who always needed to keep close eyes on the burglar and the bratty children couldn't stand to sit in the same boat with a certain someone else. They were the type of puzzles designed to quickly tell if someone was smart.

The tutors wore striped sports jerseys of red and yellow while the students who needed help donned white T-shirts with a logo bearing the same color scheme. Students who improved their grades the most wore shiny award necklaces with clinking bells.

"You get a medal just for showing up," said Roberto as he placed it around Wishy-Wishy's collar.

She took a seat and said to Roberto, "I have this book. A third of it is written in English, a third in shorthand, and a third in a language I can't recognize.

"Let me have a gander," said Roberto. He licked a finger and flipped through the pages until he came across the language Wishy-Wishy was referring to.

"You are in luck. I happen to be fluent in three languages, and Hindi is one of them."

"What are the odds?" Wishy-Wishy said.

He browsed through Adhyaksa's book and poured through the stats that Adhyaksa had gathered about the student body. "Let me tell you about room 53." His eyes grew wider. "If there are a thousand stars, the brightest stars are not the ones that shine the brightest. They are held back by such gravity that their light shines dimly. If only someone noticed; if only someone cared. But the brightest star of them all is also the dimmest because it's so far away, not in distance, but in its own dimension."

At that moment, Adrian Winklewort opened the door and said in his squeaky little voice, "Hey guys. Do you still have room for me?"

Roberto turned around and said, "If you form a line by the door, we will be with you shortly. Just keep the door open. It's starting to get warm in here." He turned around and said to Wishy-Wishy, "Now, where were we?" He looked again at Wishy-Wishy and saw the faceted irises sparkle within her eyes. They were unlike anything he had ever seen.

Wishy-Wishy saw something else. She thought she had counted ten students and twenty tutors. —But the shadows. They looked more like one hundred.

Multiple heads swayed to and fro, like those of cobras to a snake charmer. To her left and to her right she saw the head shadows of not one but three belonging to Francisco Roberto Romero.

Roberto sat fixated on Wishy-Wishy's eyes and said, "How could I have not noticed?" He looked deeper and saw, reflected back at him, all the eyes within the room, how they had multiplied a hundred times and how they twinkled in the light. "Of course. I've been blind all of this time. You have the light of a thousand eyes."

She saw the shadow of his three necks grow wider. "I don't think I can handle such flattery," said Wishy-Wishy while slowly pulling the book to herself and closing it shut. Ezequio was right. She should not have come.

"Don't be coy with me. I caught hints of your brilliance when I first laid eyes on you. It must have been what drew me to you in the first place. But what gave you away was the fact that you did not give in to the temptation of my pink lady apple."

"The ones on sale next to the kumquats?"

"Yes, third island in the produce section. Manager's special. Took me an eternity to find one that wasn't bruised."

"Do your brothers Francisco and Romero go to

this school?"

"Why yes they do," said Roberto. "We are inseparable."

"How come I've never seen them?"

"You may not have seen them, but they have always been fond of you. If ever three were one then surely we." He stood up from his chair. "At long last, brothers, our search is complete." He reached into his mouth and pulled out two rubber bands. "Do you know why I wear these retainers?"

"To prevent a crooked smile?"

He removed his retainers. "Despite my astonishingly good looks, I have a nasty overbite." He grinned and drew his gums up into his mouth to reveal his venom rich fangs which tripled in length. They all spoke as one. "It was I, Francisco Roberto Romero, the Serpent Naga Prince who bit your friend. And what's more, after I bite you, I shall be a King!"

With the book in her hands, Wishy-Wishy gob-smacked Roberto from below and sent his fangs into the bottom of his mouth. She dashed for the door and felt something strike her leg from behind but didn't have time to look. Out across the blacktops she ran. She heard a rattling whistle from behind, then countless footsteps in her pursuit.

"She will not get far without her inhaler," said

Francisco. He had pick-pocketed her just moments ago.

"Just follow your senses," said Roberto.

And thus Francisco Roberto Romero began their gentle run in pursuit of Wishy-Wishy. "We'll let the venom take effect. After all, poets are mixers of poison," said Romero.

Soon enough, Wishy-Wishy felt tired. She could not run anymore. Her sprint turned to a trot, then a walk, then a crawl into the labyrinth leading to the library. She tried to move herself with her elbows and kept low to the ground to keep out of sight. She could see the monkey-vomit-green library house near the center of the maze and hear the slithering within the bushes get closer as she cowered beneath the statue of a Minotaur. She rose to her feet and staggered again along a route she thought would lead her to the library, but she wasn't sure herself. Her left calf throbbed with pain and her left foot went lame. She tried to keep incredibly quiet, but with every step she took, the award necklace she wore around her neck made a JINGLING sound. By the time she realized her folly and looked back up from her necklace, she had walked directly to Francisco Roberto Romero who sat patiently eating a pink lady apple.

"Care for a bite of this fruit from the tree of

knowledge?" Roberto tossed the core over the hedges and pushed her to the ground. "If you want straight A's, you have to stop dragging your feet."

She tried to wrestle free as he held her down.

"One more bite should do it," said Francisco.

The stench hit Wishy-Wishy right away. She wanted to faint.

"Are my B.O.-brothers bothering you?" Roberto asked.

There was no escape. "Before I die, what is that stench? I have to know."

"You can attribute that to my yellow rat bastard brothers who ingested indigestible sewer rats in La Rambla Barcelona. And the colors on the jersey I wear, these are the colors of Catalonia."

"When identifying poisonous snakes, red meets yellow, kill a fellow, as Daddy Joe used to say. And Barcelona sits above an ancient Roman sewer. And snakes shed their skin to grow, which is exactly why you went to the spa for a skin peel. I understand now. Okay, get on with it," Wishy-Wishy said.

"I want a bite," said Romero.

"No, I want a bite," said Francisco.

"Now-now. It is only right if I get to finish her off," said Roberto. "I am the face of Francisco Roberto Romero."

"You're the face? We do all the work and you get all the glory," said Francisco.

Roberto apologized to Wishy-Wishy. "You're going to have to pardon the hissy fit. This turn-based system is not very efficient, I have to admit." He opened his mouth big and wide and held it there a few inches from her face. As digestive enzymes filled his mouth, all he could taste was a tsunami of umami.

"What are you doing? Take her!" Francisco shouted.

He couldn't do it, erase the life of this girl who taught him the fifth taste. Before umami, all he had known was the taste of sour apples, rancid ham, and bitter-sweet revenge.

"If you don't, then I will," said Romero. "You've never had it in you to be king. I have plenty of venom to give."

Wishy-Wishy grabbed her sharp # 2 pencil above her ear, the one she had been saving all school year. She aimed for Roberto —and missed. It floated in the air for a few seconds.

"AAAAGHGHGHGH," screamed Romero. His hands shot up to pull the pencil out of his eye.

Blood trickled down on the ground. Wishy-Wishy could see where the blood had painted half of Romero's face purple. He was no longer invisible. His face was inhuman, that of a green mamba.

"Now you've done it," said a voice to the left of Roberto.

Wishy-Wishy grabbed a hand full of dirt and threw it at the voice to reveal Francisco's serpentine face and forked tongue.

Just as Francisco was about to sink his fangs into Wishy-Wishy, someone tossed Francisco Roberto Romero over the hedges. It was Zepherine.

"What was that thing I just threw?" Zepherine asked.

"That was Franciso Roberto Romero, a Naga prince, a would-be king," said Wishy-Wishy. "Nagas are mythical snake people from Hindu lore." She ripped off the jingly necklace and threw it to the ground.

Zepherine handed her the end of a string.

"Follow the red string to leave the maze. It will lead you to Sean," said Samantha.

"What about you?"

"I will lead the Nagas in circles."

Samantha led a den of snakes on a wild goose chase around the maze.

Zepherine picked Wishy-Wishy up when she was too weak to walk and carried her back to the nurse's office. Moments later, Sean and Samantha came running in and barricaded the door. "How is she?" Sean asked.

"I've been bit," Wishy-Wishy said. A dark shadow grew beneath her skin. "And soon I will be forgotten. They know about room 53, Sean. They will do the same to them as they've done to Adhyaksa and me."

Zepherine set her down on a table. Her breathing grew heavy.

"Her airway is closing. She needs adrenaline," Sean said.

Wishy-Wishy gasped for air and started to go into anaphylactic shock.

"Before you forget me, say my name," Wishy-Wishy said.

"Wishy-Wishy-Woco-Mo-Loco," they all said. "We can never forget a name like that."

"Good. Thank you for remembering me. Thank you for being my friends, Sean Karcher the Archer, Samantha Atalanta, Zepherine Epherine. Go forth and save room 53 -O Pollywogs…"

Wishy-Wishy's breathing stopped. Samantha grabbed her hand. "I'm sorry I didn't believe you," Samantha said.

The room was so quiet they could hear the buzzing electric current that fed the clock on the wall. Sean held her wrist and tried to find a pulse as she started to fade into darkness.

"It is not time to call the time." Mr. Mathis said.

"Mr. Mathis. Where did you come from?" Asked Zepherine.

"You should look down sometimes. You said her name and with her last breath, she called you Zepherine-Epherine, did she not?"

Zepherine nodded, trying to hold back a teardrop that welled up in his eye. "I just can't get that song she sang yesterday out of my head. And if we are to forget her, then what does that say about us?"

"If she called you Zepherine Epherine, it could only mean one thing. If a strong boy like you was to cry, it would be tears of pure epinephrine." Mr. Mathis cupped his hands and caught a teardrop from Zepherine's chin. He poured it on Wishy-Wishy's wound. The swelling immediately shrank and the color of flesh radiated outward from the center and drove the darkness away. She drew another breath, shot up from her slumber and inhaled a deep breath of air.

"Of course," Zepherine said. Adrenaline is epinephrine and epinephrine rhymes with Zepherine."

"What happened?" Wishy-Wishy asked.

"Little Ms. Lazarus has returned," said Mr. Mathis.

"I feel cold," Wishy-Wishy said. "And who are you

calling little?"

"Well, if you're cold then go stand in the corner. It's 90 degrees."

They laughed a little, and it would have been fine if Mr. Mathis left it at that. But then he had to add, "Isn't that acute joke? Get it? Acute?"

Wishy-Wishy rolled her eyes. "Oh Mr. Mathis. 90 degrees is not an acute angle. And that wasn't a cute joke. It was more like a borderline obtuse joke." She realized her mistake in being correct when she saw Mr. Mathis shrink from the size of a guinea pig to the size of a hamster. "Oh my! I'm so sorry, Mr. Mathis."

"You needn't apologize. I should have known better," said Mr. Mathis.

"No more math jokes," Everyone yelled.

"Alright, alright. Sheesh." Mr. Mathis got on the school intercom. "Attention Lewis Middle School staff and student body. We have a snake situation that will require you to shelter in place. Repeat. Shelter in place. Barricade the doors. Do not let any snake-like beings slither into class unless cleared to do so by staff. Thank you for your cooperation and happy learning and pee in your pants if you have to."

Wishy-Wishy got up and limped on her own power. She could feel her strength slowly returning. She placed a hand on Samantha's shoulder to brace herself and said, "We have a problem with these snake people. Nagas, as they should be called, are running around and biting people. We have no way of knowing who's been bitten. I venture to guess that once the poison kicks in and the shadow envelops them, they will have been forgotten."

"That's right," Samantha agreed.

Then Wishy-Wishy realized that Adhyaksa had already taken the time to catalogue all the sixth graders in shorthand. She reached into her bag and pulled out Adhyaksa's journal. She read through the names of some of the kids. She read the names of Annabelle Thompson and Rahil Gupta, and when nobody recognized them, she stopped. They knew that a person had been forgotten. "Whoever they were, they must have been someone's friends. This book is our only link to those we have forgotten."

"Then we must keep it safe," Sean said. He searched through the drawers and found an unused one-gallon resealable plastic bag and gave it to Wishy-Wishy.

"How will we defeat the Nagas?" Zepherine asked.

"Are you not Zepherine Epherine?" Mr. Mathis asked. Well don't just stand by the standpipe on standby."

Zepherine placed his hands on the four-inch pipe

running down the wall and looked back at Mr. Mathis.

"Don't worry, there's nothing in it." Mr. Mathis said.

Zepherine squeezed the pipe with ease. It was like silly putty in his hands. He removed it from the wall and made a pretzel.

"Wishy-Wishy has given you the strength to move mountains," said Mr. Mathis. He turned to Samantha. "Samantha Atalanta. You have the speed of the legendary sprinter…Atatlanta, of course. And Sean Karcher the Archer, you should be able to shoot a fly off an apple on somebody's head with a bow and arrow."

"For real?" Sean asked.

"Let's find out," said Mr. Mathis. "Samantha, I want you to mosey on over to the athletic supply room and fetch a bow and arrow set for Sean. Bring back plenty of arrows."

They peeked outside, and when nobody was around, Samantha ran out the door and returned with the goods in four seconds.

"Presto!" Samantha said.

Sean Karcher the Archer shot the bow and arrow and nicked a worm off the narrows of a sparrow's pointy beak.

Mr. Mathis rolled out a potato he had taken from a

science fair battery project. "We must fight them with literal weapons. Sean. Help me dice up these spuds to make cubed roots. When placed on the tip of an arrow, it will shrink the target by a cubic factor." Next, he tore out the first few pages from an old William Faulkner book. "Samantha. Help me grind this into a fine powder. I never understood Faulkner nor do I want to waste my life trying. Throw this Faulkner dust onto the enemy to slow and confuse them."

"I feel so much better hearing that from you," said Wishy-Wishy.

"Who's Faulkner?" Samantha asked.

Mr. Mathis looked at Samantha and said, "I pray you never have to read him, dear child. You don't need to prove anything to an English Lit snob. Do yourself a favor and jump straight to the Cliff Notes. One does not exactly use William Faulkner in a pick-me-up line either. 'Hey girl, do you want to skip the movies and read some *As I lay Dying* with me at the DMV?' I tried it on Ms. Gertrude. She almost stepped on me."

Not a moment too soon did they hear Roberto's taunting voice over the P.A. stem. "Wishy…Wishy -where are you?"

"They've broken into my office," Mr. Mathis said.

Then they heard a crying scream.

"We have something that belongs to you, Wishy-Wishy. And in the middle of the quad, we have the sun."

"Oh no. Roberto knows about Ezequio's weakness," Wishy-Wishy said. "He's alone out there and he's helpless. We have to save him."

"You will bring Mr. Mathis to open room 53, else your squonk will meet the sun," said Roberto.

CHAPTER 18

THE EAGLE KING

As she walked through the silent hallways, curious students looked on through classroom windows and wondered why she was the only one out and about. She saw Francisco Roberto Romero standing over a slumping Ezequio in front of room 53. Ezequio sat along the wall holding a limp arm. Wishy-Wishy could see a raised lump where the Nagas had bitten him.

"This is the key to room 53," Mr. Mathis said as Wishy-Wishy handed it to Roberto.

Just as Roberto opened the door, an arrow zipped across the quad and pinned his hand to the wall. Samantha Atalanta threw Faulkner dust on the Nagas while cubed root arrows from Sean Karcher the Archer shrank some Nagas down to size. Zepherine Epherine jumped down from the rooftop and fought off a team of Nagas to defended the classroom.

"Run Wishy run!" Zepherine shouted.

More Nagas came up from the swamps,

surrounded room 53, and cluttered the corridors. They moved from side to side, yet forward in an unpredictable way. Wishy-Wishy stood frozen and didn't know what to do. It was then that Ezequio stepped out from the shadows and held out his hand. And so Wishy-Wishy took Ezequio's hand and ran with him for one last time across the quad and in the scorching sun.

"What are you doing?" Wishy-Wishy asked. "You're burning."

He looked at her and didn't say anything, but winced.

With all the exits blocked, there was nowhere to go but to the church building. They ran across the aisles, through the vestibule, and up the spiral stairs to the bell tower. Wishy-Wishy locked the door, but it was a mistake. The whole church idea was a big mistake. Within the bell tower, there was little shade to be had. It was open on all four sides. There was nothing between them and the honest light of day. Francisco Roberto Romero waited patiently below.

By then, most of the mud had flaked off. There was too much ambient light. No matter how she tried, she could not block out the sun. Ezequio laid on his back and soaked up the sun. And even as he burned, he started to shiver from the venom coursing through his veins.

"We have to get you out of the sun," Wishy-Wishy said.

He reached out a hand and felt Wishy-Wishy's face. "One shade the more. One ray the less."

She blushed, but she didn't know why.

"I'm sorry," Ezequio said. His breathing grew heavy and rapid. "I wanted more than anything to be your sunshine, to cheer for you in your moments of triumph. Wishy-Wishy. Wocomoloco."

It was then that Wishy-Wishy realized what Ezequio was to her all along. The time he poured chocolate milk on her and kept her from winning the spelling bee, the homework he ripped in two to keep her from getting the best grade in class, the mud that he had splashed on her yellow dress and smeared on her face, he was trying to deflect positive attention away from her, masking her popularity in embarrassment, hoping that the Jabberwock or his minions would think less of her.

"All this time, you were just trying to protect me. And for that, I turned you into a squonk." She removed from her hair the braided barrette that Sean had made for her and placed it on Ezequio as a crown.

A teardrop landed on Ezequio's face. It came from Mr. Mathis, but it was a teardrop nonetheless. "Darn.

I tried to beat you to the punch, but nothing happened," said Mr. Mathis.

"I'm supposed to be one who's crying," said Wishy-Wishy. And so her eyes too welled up with tears of joy for the happiest times she spent with him, and tears of sadness for the fate she had given him. She let flow a shower that landed on Ezequio. It washed away the mud to reveal unborn skin to the sun. She saw him again for a moment. She ran her fingers across his face. She wanted to take in every detail, what he looked like before the mud, what he felt like before his face melted away in the cruel, cruel sun. "I will never forget you, Ezequio Magnifico."

He writhed in pain, fell off the bell tower and landed in a smoldering heap.

"Ezequio!" Wishy-Wishy yelled from above. She wanted to jump after him, but Mr. Mathis held her back, one hand gripping the edge of the bell and another one locked on a lock of her hair. It knelled four times, sending its sounds throughout the town, shaking Mr. Mathis to his core like never before. His eyes wobbled and spun in opposite directions.

A dry gust of wind formed a dozen dirt devils that merged with each other and encircled Ezequio's body. It caught fire and grew hotter and hotter, making the Nagas withdraw. From this inferno arose a fireball of red and gold. It rode the heat of a restless day, straight into the air, so high that it blocked out the sun. No. It was as if the sun had wings.

"I was mistaken," Mr. Mathis said. "He is not a squonk. He is Garuda the Eagle King and the sun is what powers him."

Fire raced up the bell tower. The Eagle King landed on the precipice and flapped his majestic wings for Wishy-Wishy to climb on his back. The laurel crown became the reins. She hung on tight and dared not open her eyes as they soared to the skies and swept back down. The Eagle King grabbed the Nagas into the air with his talons and ripped them in two. "One for me and one for you," said the Eagle King before sending their slimy innards to the ground. He continued his aerial campaign until no student was in any danger of getting bitten. Only then did he take back to the skies and circled about, surveying the campus with his sharp eyes.

Roberto tried to run away, but it did not look pleasurable. He panted heavily, and the sweat that emanated from his pores exposed parts of his scaly scalp.

"You shall not hurt my students!" Mr. Mathis shouted as The Eagle King dive-bombed Roberto from behind, grabbed hold of Francisco and Romero' invisible heads, lifted them into the air and ripped them to shreds and threw them visibly across the ground. Roberto slumped to his knees. Purple blood trickled and squirted from his twitching shoulders.

"You can open your eyes now," said the Eagle King to Wishy-Wishy.

"Just finish me off," Roberto quipped.

"No," said Wishy-Wishy. "Two heads are better than one. But three can be telling. You will make your own decisions now. No one will tell you what's right or wrong."

"Come to think of it, I feel like a burden has been lifted from my shoulders. You've freed me of my separation anxiety. I'm sorry I lied to you Wishy-Wishy. Grown men with fancy leather jackets in their prime working-age don't actually like to play hide the marble along La Rambla. It is not Catalonia's national pastime. Pick-pocketing? That's another story."

"I already knew that," said Wishy-Wishy. How fun could it be? What are the odds? One in three?"

Roberto let out a coughing chuckle. "Smart as always, Wishy-Wishy-Woco-Mo-Loco. Please forgive my past transgressions." He handed Wishy-Wishy back her inhaler.

"Thanks, but no thanks," Wishy-Wishy said. "I no longer have asthma."

"I will call off the Naga attack, but know this. The school you return to tomorrow will not be the same. And moreover, you did have a friend. Her name was Adhyaksa."

"I know," Wishy-Wishy said while glancing at the Eagle King. I've always had a friend. So why did you bite me, Roberto?"

"It's just that the Jabberwock said I would be a seven-headed Naga King if I delivered to him the light of a thousand eyes, someone like you. It was hard enough with three heads. Can you imagine seven? At first, I thought that was what I wanted. But after living in the real world, more than anything, I wanted to be human, like you and your friends. And now, for failing miserably, I will fade into the imaginary realm where I belong." Roberto took a whistle from his pocket and blew on it with his last breath. It sounded more like a rattle than a whistle. He choked on something in his throat, then spat out a half-digested yellow rat before falling to the ground.

"You will not be forgotten, Roberto Cierto. I can't un-smell that. Thank you for telling me the truth," Wishy-Wishy said.

"I will take you home now," said the Eagle King. They took back to the skies and flew west. From that day on, snakes only had one head and sought shelter beneath the earth, always wary of the Eagle King circling above.

Wishy-Wishy peered to the north and saw what looked like a neoclassical college campus. "Is that the forgotten realm?"

"It's where all the brightest students end up. It can take on many forms but it is not visible to normal eyes. There are few who can imagine it. Only those who have been bitten can see it." Mr. Mathis replied. "Although in my days, it was vampires who did the biting."

"Ezequio, I'm glad you are not Icarus," Wishy-Wishy said.

"Why so?" He asked.

"Because your wings would have been made of wax and if you dared to achieve wonderful things and soar to such great heights, they would melt from the heat of the sun."

Wishy-Wishy ran her fingers through his feathers, straightened out the veins and patted down the downs. She felt his warm wing muscles flexing and contracting beneath, each beat producing a gust of wind that propelled them up and forward a few hundred feet before descending to the next beat.

The school buildings looked little toy train cars and paled in comparison to the ones she saw to the north.

And although the view was pretty, she closed her eyes for a spell and took in the sights of that happy moment when she flew across the breezeways on the back of her muddy squonk. She thought of a school she once knew and was no more. She already missed the stories Mr. Mathis had yet to tell in class. She missed a world that would not remember Adhyaksa. But most of all, she missed how Adhyaksa would pause to smile between saying things as if it were a comma or purse her lips in place of semicolons.

"I'm all for smaller classroom sizes, but this is taking things a bit too far," said Mr. Mathis. He sat on Wishy-Wishy's shoulder and clung to a lock of hair.

Wishy-Wishy noticed that even in godlike Garuda form, Ezequio was still wounded. Each beat of his wings grew more labored.

"Maybe if I tell a bad joke I can shrink and we can fly farther," Mr. Mathis said.

"Save it. Not to belittle you, but your jokes are really lame." She turned to Ezequio and said, "I know now why you cried on the first day of school. They were tears for your mother, were they not?"

"Yes."

"What was her name?"

"Sonia. Her family name is Ferreira. I carry it as my middle name. We're from Portugal."

"So your full name is Ezequio Ferreira Reis."

"I have a great memory, but only for the things that matter. That is the gift she gave to me."

"Then we must find her."

"And Adhyaksa too."

She noticed his wings beating harder. "Are you tired? You don't have to carry me home. Just land somewhere and we can walk the rest of the way."

"Is that your house over there?" The Eagle King asked.

"Yes. That would be my cozy home. I can see it. It's just beyond the primrose hills," Wishy-Wishy answered.

"It's nice you have a place you can still call home."

He must have misjudged either the distance or the time of day for the sun was close to setting, and perhaps the powers it had conferred upon him was also waning as they passed the line of trees and glided across the long lake toward a log in a bog that was Wishy-Wishy's home.

"I forgot to mention," Mr. Mathis said. "Saying his full name will undo the spell."

"Now you tell me," said Wishy-Wishy.

"As they say in life, it's all about the timing, and my timing couldn't be worse."

Feathers blew off in greater successions as the tiny

house came closer into view. Ezequio could not make it. His wings turned back to arms and hands, talons back to legs and feet.

They plunged into the eggshell lake. Ezequio was too exhausted to swim and never had a buoyant personality to begin with. He would have sunken to the depths alone, but Wishy-Wishy hung on tight and would not let him go. Try as she might, her hand could only parse the waters or mince it with her fingers. So she too sank with him, along with a tiny Mr. Mathis who was powerless to resist the undertow between cold and colder that dragged them down into the darkness.

Wishy-Wishy laid on the bottom of the lake, arm clutched to Ezequio, the last few bubbles rising in a direction that must have been up. Her lungs burned. She saw a huge alligator flagellate above and wanted to scream to the man-eater for help but couldn't. *This can't be it,* she thought. *I'd like to pay the Jabberwock a visit...and slay him... If only the gator could get me in a spiral death grip, render me to tatters, maybe I can get one last breath of air.*

Her heart grew heavy. Her chest was about to relax when she saw streaks of clarity from above. And what long light remained of the day danced across the Milky Way and rained down in helical rivulets of amber and gold. A female form undulated in the distance. A bolt of hair ran down the length of this curvy maid, and where she swam within the lake, crystal waters followed within her wake. She reached behind and unraveled her spiral braid. The alligator accompanied her and gave her a seat. And as they circled in the vortex, the water wicked and vanished into the void of her dark, dark hair. What depths of water remained spun round and round like a walled river with no beginning and no end.

Wishy-Wishy coughed out a lung full of water and then looked up or was it down? The waters no longer pressed her chest. If it weren't for the sticky mud, she felt like she would have fallen into an aubergine sky.

The long-haired lady stepped off the alligator and said, "This is my often misunderstood friend."

"Who are you?" Wishy-Wishy asked while catching her breath.

"Who am I? You of all people should know." She sent tendrils from her temples into the mouths of Ezequio and Mr. Mathis, siphoning out the brackish water while filling their lungs with air. The two coughed out hairballs like cats after a long day of fur licking.

"I have to admit," the lady went on. "When I came to my senses after jumping into the river, I was mad at the shallowness. I was mad at you for calling me Lucretia of the Black Lagoon. I found it almost insulting. But in life, it is the name that often chooses you and not the other way around. So I followed to the tributary to see where it may lead. I spoke with the swamp creatures and lost my dreadful British accent. No matter how dark the waters became, I learned to focus on the positive feelings that I alone can create. The better I got at it, the clearer the waters that followed my wake until my name took on new meaning and the Earth Goddess I became." She let out a sigh. "Though I am in need of a salon." The tendrils lifted everyone into the air. "Now climb onto my friend. We weren't always a pair, but we have come to an arrangement."

The twenty-foot reptile ambled along the muddy bottoms and snapped up croaking catfish and gaping largemouth bass into its formidable jaws. Only when her friend had satiated himself and said, "Gator done," did Lucretia lean to one side of the alligator and twist her hair to squeeze out the water it had consumed. She brought everyone back to the surface. The vortex dissolved into the frothy stillness of a lake at moonrise.

"Now tell me where it is you wish to go."

"Home," Wishy-Wishy said. "Take us home."

❈ ❈ ❈

THE END

CPSIA information can be obtained
at www.ICGtesting.com
Printed in the USA
LVHW091631210820
663838LV00004B/599